Prologue

Nothing that she could have ever imagined would have stopped what happened. She stood over his body knowing what she had done. This was inevitable. She tried for years on ways to make him not do what he had done for so long. She thought that he would change. She thought that she would be the one to make him change. But he did not change. He just got smarter about how he did it. That is probably why she snapped. She did not think that it would come to this but it did. Now he is dead, and she has no way to fix it.

She searched for a way to get his body out of the house. Joshua was such a big guy in comparison to her. She still did not understand how she could overpower him. He was six foot eight and three hundred pounds compared with her five foot one and one hundred and thirty-two-pound frame. But after his all-night drinking binge and his continuous sexual abuse of her that evening, he was just too wasted to even put up a good fight. She just still stood over him trying to figure out how she could get to the side table drawer and light him up with those three bullets center mast like she was taught by her dad during his law enforcement training.

There was only one person she could think of calling and that was her dad; Felton. Felton was an ex-CIA agent who spent his days considering cold cases for the Pittsburgh Gang Task Force and his nights smoking joints and having escapades with ladies younger than his 36-year-old daughter. It was only natural that when she phoned

him, he was there within thirty minutes. Amber was pacing the floor at a speed that would be considered a slow sprint rather than a nervous walk. Her father called her name several times before she even realized he was in the house and standing several feet away from Joshua's still warm body. When she saw her father, all she could do was let out a small moan and fall to the floor. "I will make some calls, but first you have to tell me what happened. You have to start from the beginning," said Felton as he embraced his daughter on the floor. "Well," Amber says as she takes a deep breath between sobs and her face just went stiff; and the silence in the room was broken by a blood-curdling scream-like noise from Joshua's body on the bedroom floor.

Chapter 1

Running-That is all she knew how to do was run. She would run at night, and she would run in the day. Her days were spent trying to get faster. It did not matter that she was on a full scholarship from Xavier University for track as she was determined to go to the Olympics one day. Amber Hollingsworth was the girl that everyone wanted. It did not matter if they were male or female; they wanted her. But who could blame them. She was short but her legs were still long. She had eyes that were like gray wading pools. She got those from her mom's side of the family. Her dad's side of the family gave her full lips with long dark dirty brown hair and a beautiful singing voice. She was not only beautiful and one of the fastest runners in all Upstate New York but also smart. She was the valedictorian of her high school in Westchester County. No one could touch her in the classroom or on the track. So, it was not a surprise when she got the academic and athletic scholarships from Xavier University. They were the only ones to offer her a double scholarship, even though she had over fifty offers from various schools. That made her parents very happy because they knew how much Amber wanted to be in the medical field-a neurosurgeon to be exact.

Amber had her fill of running on this fall day. It was an unusually hot day in New Orleans for it to be this time of the year. The leaves were turning a beautiful shade of auburn, and the wind was blowing a slightly warm breeze. But for some reason, Amber felt as if she was on fire. She was dressed to the nines and looked stunning as she slowed her sprinting to a jog. She looked around the campus of

Xavier University and wondered what her classes would bring her that day. She knew that being in premed was just the start to being the neurosurgeon that she promised her grandmother she would one day be. "Your hands are made to change lives" is what her Grandmother used to tell her. But she never believed that. "Your feet will not only win the race but also walk you right into your destiny," her Grandmother Anne Marie would also say. But Amber's feet were used to keep her out of trouble more than once in her life. She did not know that one day, it would possibly save her.

"Chick, did you see the way he was looking at you?" asked Cheyanne. "No, child. I am not paying his ass any mind. I am so sick of Benjamin! What makes him think I am like Rayland at all? I am not an airhead or naïve," says Amber as she sucked her teeth and sipped on her Sprite. "Benjamin wants to holler girl. So, what is the problem?" says Cheyanne as she adjusts her breasts. "If you do not holler at him then I will," "Well go ahead, because we both know that you will put out before I will," says Amber jokingly. "Man, forget you. You are such a prude!" says Cheyanne as she struts towards Benjamin.

Benjamin Holmes was something to look at. He was a fine yellow bone with hazel eyes and curly jet black hair. Standing at a mere six foot eleven and wearing a size 12.5 shoe, he made some of the guys at Towson Catholic High look like elves that were suffering from malnutrition. Not only was he tall, but also he had the muscles to back it up. He was an All-American football player and basketball player. The girls went crazy over him, but he knew that all he had to do was look at them and they would drop their panties. Unfortunately, he was

a player and his almost ex-girlfriend, Rayland Striker, knew it. They were on and off since freshman year; but it seemed like this time, they were through; and she let him know she could do whatever she wanted with whoever she wanted to do it with. Benjamin was known for his hit-it-and-quit-it routine, but this did not keep the girls from beating down his door. It was junior year and every girl was trying to be his lady for the Homecoming and ultimately the Junior Prom. But he had eyes for Amber, and she was not having it whatsoever.

"So what's good, daddy?" Cheyanne says flirting with Benjamin. "Ain't nothing Cheyanne. Trying to get your girl's attention, but she is not even budging," says Benjamin with annoyance in his deep husky voice. The sound of the rumbling of his voice through the quad made Cheyanne shiver in all her private places. "Yeah. I think she just might not be interested. I know someone who would be," Cheyanne says while taking a slow lick of her lollipop as she gazes up at Benjamin. He could not help but look and stare as she maneuvers her tongue around every inch of that lollipop. He was thinking what would it would be like if he was with Cheyanne instead.

Cheyanne Louis was nothing but the truth. Cheyanne and Amber had been friends since the sixth grade. They were the ones to hang with. They not only were athlete/scholars but also were popular and good looking. Cheyanne stood at around five foot seven and was a milk chocolate island girl who had long eyelashes with big brown eyes. She wore all the latest styles; and it helped that her father, who was from Barbados, owned almost every laundry mat on the lower East Side of New York. So, Cheyanne's family was well off. Cheyanne used

her luscious lips and those nice bow legs to get whatever she wanted from whoever she wanted. She danced, she cheered, and she ran track just like her friend; but she was bad to the bone. Cheyanne had an addiction to bad boys and sex. And she was determined to make Benjamin another notch on her belt, by any means necessary.

Amber watched as Cheyanne flirted with Benjamin. She laughed and thought about how shameful it was to be throwing yourself at a guy who was in high school. She always thought Benjamin was a fine specimen of a high school man, but she did not have time for his shenanigans. She had her thoughts on something bigger and better - her next-door neighbor Morales. Morales Brown was who she wanted, and she was surely going to get him. She fantasized about kissing his cute little lips. His whole demeanor and swag reminded her of Tupac in his younger days. She knew that getting with him would be a problem. He was older than her, but she did not know by how much because they never had a real conversation with each other besides the neighborly "hello" when they saw each other outside of their homes. Amber watched him, and she wondered if he noticed how much she did. He was not the kind of guy people would expect her to be with because he was short like her and she had a disdain for short guys. She always talked to guys at least five foot ten or taller, but he was only five foot seven. This was an unusual thing for her; but once she set her mind on something, she usually got it and she wanted Morales.

Amber got off the bus and was walking home with Cheyanne. They were gossiping as usual. Suddenly, Amber hears a familiar sound. It is the sound of Morales' Magnum coming down the street at fu

speed. The sight of the car made Amber's heart flutter. She never felt like this for anyone that she never had that much interaction with before. She was not sure the feelings she was starting to feel in other regions of her body also. She noticed that when they would catch each other's glances for brief periods, things would happen to her physically that would cause her to break eye contact quickly. Morales pulled right up next to them on the sidewalk and Amber dropped her books. Morales jumped out of his car and picked them up.

"Oh man. I did not mean to scare you little mamma. I was just trying to get your attention," Morales says as he hands her back her books. "It is okay," Amber says trying to act cool about it and not let him see her blushing. "I wanted to talk to you about something. Could I give you a ride to the house and we can talk?" Morales said as he looked Amber right in the eyes and this made her almost drop her books again. "Yeah that will be cool. Cheyanne, I will call you later okay?" Amber said as she got into his car. "Hey wait. Why can't I get a ride, too?" Cheyanne yelled as they were about to pull off. Morales let Amber's window down and yelled, "Nope, little mamma. I heard about you. I don't want them to think I am into threesomes with little girls." He smirked and drove off as Cheyanne gave him the finger.

The music blared. The wind was blowing Amber's hair in her face. All Amber could do was sit stiff as a board in Morales' car to keep from throwing up. She did not know what to do or what to say. She always imagined what it would be like to be in his presence more than just in passing by. She never imagined being in his car with him and being driven home. He was talking to her, and she did not even hear

him until he touched her arm and she almost jumped out of his car's window. "You must have bad nerves little roadrunner!" Morales said as he laughed. "You almost jumped out of your skin. What were you thinking about?" "Oh nothing. Just chilling and enjoying the ride," she said nervously. "What did you want to talk to me about, Morales?"

He pulled into his yard and turned off the ignition. He turned and looked at her. "I noticed that you have been watching me. I was wondering why? Aren't you like in eleventh-grade?" Morales says as he brushes Amber's hair out of her face. She does not know how to reply. She just sits there and looks at her Jordan's. "Well I know for a fact that you are not a mute. I know you can sing because you make it your duty to start singing or making a lot of noise when you take the garbage out at your house, which is right by my bedroom window; so, I know you have a voice somewhere in that little head of yours. So, answer me and tell me what's up little roadrunner." "I do not know what to say. I have been watching you since you and your friends were in front of your house dressed in all white for Delroy's funeral last month. All this time that we have lived next door to each other, I never paid you any attention until that day. I am not sure why," Amber says never taking her eyes off her shoes.

"I think you should look me in my face and tell me what you have going on in that mind of yours. But before you do, I am going to let you out of the car so you can go home and think about what it is that you want to say to me. Then write it down because, I have learned that writing down things sometimes comes out better when you are having a hard time wrapping such soft-looking lips around the words,

Morales says as he leans over and kisses Amber on the cheek. "Just remember you are seven years younger than me, so this is all about what you want. I am not forcing you. But just know I have been watching recently also, and I sure do like what I see. Run on home Shorty. We will talk soon, hopefully. If not, I will listen for you to serenade me at the garbage cans." Amber opened the car door slowly and looked up at Morales. She gave him a shy smile, gathered her things, and exited the car. She ran as fast as she could to her house, unlocked the side door that led directly to her bedroom, opened it, locked it back, and plopped on her bed. She laid there as her belongings fell from her arms and hands and tried to figure out what the hell just happened to her. What would she do about it?

Chapter 2

Amber went about her night as normal as she could, but she just could not get Morales out of her head. She contemplated every word he said to her, and she did not know how to respond. It frustrated her so badly that she just did not tell him how she felt. But knowing how much older he was not only frightened her but also excited her. Chills ran down her spine as she thought about the sensuous kiss he laid on her cheek. Even when she showered after she got home from school, she refrained from any water touching her face. She knew before the night was over though that she had to clean it with her face scrub. Even still, she wondered what she would say in her letter to him.

Amber laid across her bed to figure out what she should write to Morales. Her head was clouded with so many thoughts at one time. She wanted to sound mature when she wrote how she felt on paper but she did not know if her book smarts would play out in such an intimate matter. She turned over on her back and stared up at the ceiling, and she pondered of the smell of Morales when he leaned over to kiss her on her cheek. A pulsating sensation down below sent a twitch in her chest. Her breathing changed. This was a feeling that she never felt before. Her palms began to sweat, and she was not sure what this feeling was that she had. She knew that this must be lust or something. She heard from Cheyanne about what it felt like when she got all hot and bothered; but because Amber was still a virgin, she had no clue how this would feel. It was just the case that she was only one of three girls that were in their little click who had not done the deed.

Amber was not sure of what she should do because the more she thought of Morales, the more excited her lower part seemed to get. She felt the urge to do something that Cheyanne had showed her at one of their sleepovers. They did a lot of experimenting with each other where Cheyanne would show how her how she would self-pleasure herself, and they have kissed before but never had Amber ever touched another person or herself in a sexual manner. The feelings that she was having because of her unclean thoughts of Morales made her so excited, yet nervous at the same time. She wanted to relieve herself of this what she thought of as built-up pressure in a ready-to-burst pipe, but she did not want to do the things that she watched Cheyanne do to herself. She wanted Morales to do it. She wondered what it would feel like to be touched by him down there. She tried to shake the thoughts, but they came back. She took advantage of her thoughts and wrote them down on a piece of paper. The words flowed through her so fast like the raging rapids to the notepad. The longer she sat there, the more she had these thoughts and the longer the letter got. When she finished, she had written 5 pages.

She folded the letter and placed it in an envelope she found in her mom's room. Her mom, Leslie, always had some stationary and envelopes on her desk. Leslie Baptiste-Pryor worked as book editor for an international publishing company since she decided to stop teaching, and she was consistently mailing and receiving transcripts of some sort. Amber used one of her mom's perfumes to spray the envelope. She saw Cheyanne do this with a letter she sent to a pen pal she made with this guy in the State Penitentiary. Amber thought that

was so weird, but Cheyanne was the black sheep of their group anyway. Amber ran as fast as she could to the kitchen and grabbed the garbage.

"And where are you going young lady smelling like you are going on a date?" says Leslie as she looked at her daughter's flushed face. "I am going to take out the trash before I run down to Cheyanne's house. I have to borrow a book for school from her," Amber says while tying a knot in the bag. "Okay pumpkin. Just let her brother walk you back home if it is after dark okay?" Leslie said with concern in her voice. "Ok," Amber yelled as she ran out of the door.

When the back door slammed, Amber tried to compose herself for what she did not know would happen or not. All she knew was that she was going to get this letter to Morales and let him know that she wanted him to deflower her. She knew the risks, but she did not care. She was tired of being harassed for being one of the few left in the group who was still a virgin. She did not want to be lost anymore when the girls talked about the orgasms that they did or did not have. He was still confused about whether she would like to get or give what they called "head." Amber was just sick and tired of being treated like an outcast or defected when she dated guys and would not give it up. She was either condemned or pitied for being the "good girl." Now, she wanted a piece and that would be where Morales came into play.

Amber started strolling towards the side of the house where the garbage cans were kept. She began to sing as usual. She loved the Fantasia song "When I See You," and she felt that it was an appropriate one to sing when you were trying to get someone to ge

with you so to speak. She walked as slowly as she could to get to the garbage. She waited and then placed the bag in the garbage can. She turned around and looked right into Morales' bedroom window. He was not there. Or was he?

When she turned around to replace the can's top and turned back to start to leave to Cheyanne's house, Morales was standing right there. "So what did you decide little roadrunner?" Morales said with the sexiest mixture of a Dominican and New York accent. She never noticed it until just then. She blushed and handed him the note. "It is all there and you can read it when you are ready," Amber said trying to sound like she had done this before. She felt an air of confidence.

Morales started towards Amber. She became quite nervous. She did not know what to do. She was thinking that she should run. He could not catch her if she did. He placed his body against hers. "I am going to read this, but I want to in front of you," he says as he opens the letter. He begins to read; and after every paragraph, he looked up at her and right into her eyes. Amber never had a guy look at her the way he had at that very moment. She felt wanted and not just sexually. "I have never had a girl nor woman ever say these things to me that you have. The maturity of what you wrote in this so far has me in a state of awe and deep desire. I thought that this would be just a little game and you would probably just say something silly that would make me end this. But now, I just want to hold you. Is that okay?" Morales asks and steps back to give Amber her space. "I want you to do more than that. I want to feel you here," Amber says as she takes Morales by the hand and places it on her lower region.

"No," Morales says and backs further away. Amber looks confused. She looked defeated. "Not here. Not now. But when you are ready. But I will leave you with this," says Morales as he places his lips on her neck. He caresses her bottom in his hands as he kisses her softly and gently on her neck. The more he kisses her, the more she becomes flustered in more ways than one. He moves his hand from her bottom to her breasts and slides them down her abdomen. Morales kisses Amber passionately on her lips and goes to place his hand where no man has gone before but her doctor. He stops. He whispers into her ear, "Not now. Not here. But when you are truly ready." He kisses her again and goes into the house. Amber stands against the house for at least two minutes before darting off to Cheyanne's house. Boy, does she have a lot to talk to her about.

"He did what? Oh, my gosh. You let him? You wanted him? Did you let him smash?" Cheyanne asks Amber questions in the speed of an automatic pitching machine at a batting range. "Man, female slow down with all the questions and just listen. Dude came at me with the fact that he knew I was watching him, and he wanted me to write my feelings down. But the more I thought about him," Amber's voice trailed off as she sat down on Cheyanne's bed. "I got kind of excited. The kind of excited that you told me about and showed me the last time I slept over. I thought you were full of it until I almost touched myself. So, I started writing and I kept writing until I almost imploded. Girl and then that's when I went outside and it almost went down!"

Cheyanne stared at Amber in amazement. She never thought that Amber would ever cross that line with any guy until she go

married. She knew that Amber came from a very strict Haitian Catholic family; and even though Amber's family moved to Upstate New York from Georgia when Amber was in middle school, her mom ensured that she would continue to raise her that Catholic way. Amber's family moved there after her stepfather mysteriously died. There was never a clue as in to how he died, but her mom just decided she could not take living in Atlanta anymore. Cheyanne just could not take her eyes off Amber. She stared at her like a proud mom watching her infant walking for the first time.

"So what should I do?" asks Cheyanne. Amber sits up straight, "What do you mean by what should you do? I want to have sex with him, but I think he wants to have a relationship. And you know what? I am down. But how is this going to work?" Cheyanne paces the floor. "Well you know your mom is always at church or work, and you got me. You know my mom is always at work or sleeping, and she lets me do whatever. She never comes down the hall unless she needs me to curl her hair. So y'all can kick it in my room. I would love to watch!" Cheyanne says jokingly as she sits down on the bed by Amber. "Do you need any tips?" "Not from you, you are a slut bag," Amber laughs back at Cheyanne. Cheyanne is not amused at all. She folds her arms in complete disdain for what Amber said. "I am offended," Cheyanne said annoyingly. "You should be. But now you can most definitely kick it to Benjamin because I am off the market officially," Amber says as she gets up to leave. "I have a real man now!" Amber sashays her way out of Cheyanne's room with a new kind of swing that made Cheyanne's head snap back. "Well, look at you miss thing!" Cheyanne

says as she jumps up and pops her lips while rolling her eyes at Amber as she leaves her house. "Walk her home big brother!" Cheyanne yells to her big brother, Tim, who leaves out of his door as he hears Amber starting to leave. "Alright!" Tim says with an attitude.

Amber thanks Tim for riding her home on his bike, and she starts to walk to her house. She has a feeling like she is being watched. She looks around but does not see anyone. She goes to her door that leads to her room from the outside and puts her key in the lock. Suddenly, she is pushed against the door and a hand covers her mouth. She could feel the person's breath on the back of her neck. But they smelled so familiar. She tried to struggle but the person was very strong. The person used their other hand to rub her from her shoulder blade to her breast. The person took their hand and fondled her breast She began to cry.

"Wait, don't cry. I just wanted to surprise you. I thought i would be cute or funny. I don't know. I am sorry!" Morales says as he turns her around and tries to hug her. She slapped him with all her might. She tries to hit him again, but he catches her hand in midair and pulls her towards him. He hugs her again and keeps whispering that he was sorry in her ear. Her body is less tense now, and she calms down "If you know what happened to me when I was younger, you would never have done that. But you don't know me. So how could you want someone you don't know? How could you want me?" Amber say through tears. "You should ask yourself the same question I believe," Morales says as he wipes her face with the back of his hand, kisses her and walks towards his house. He turns and mouths "I am sorry."

Chapter 3

Amber unlocks her room door and quickly goes inside. She locks the door behind her and proceeds to cry. She throws herself onto her bed and cries for about an hour. How could he do that? Why would he do that? These thoughts and others were tearing through her mind. She did not know what to think or where to even start her thought process, but all she knew was that she was rethinking her feelings for him. She began to remove her clothes so that she could go to bed. A note fell out of her pocket. She picked it up and wondered where it had come from. She looked it over and on the other side it said: "To the one I hope to call my boo." She smiled through dried tears. It was from Morales. She went back to her bed and opened it and began to read it.

"I never thought that I would be writing to someone so young like you. But to be honest, I can see why guys are always trying to talk to you. You are not easy, so that is attractive but also quite annoying to young cats. But for me, it is nothing because you know I have a daughter, so I have obviously had relations before. Anyways, I just wanted to let you know that I will not do anything that you want. I just want to be what it is you said in the note you want me to be. I want to be the one that you give your most precious gift to but not rush it. I can help you get to that point but on your own terms. This will work out somehow, but we must be a team. There is a lot at risk for what we are about to enter into. Be ready for anything. Call me 555-9876, and we can talk. Bye my sweet. Morales."

Amber was at a loss for words. She quickly pulled out her iPhone 6s and texted the number he gave her. She had to let him know that everything was okay and that she was not ready to tell him why what he did upset her so much. If he only knew what made her react the way she did. Any other normal girl may have been alright with what he did, but she was not a normal girl. At least she was not a normal girl, psychologically, because of what happened to her back home in Atlanta. But she was not going to let what happened back then to stop her from getting with Morales. Amber waited patiently for a return text. Within one minute, Morales texted her back, "I am sorry and I will never scare you again like that. When you are ready to tell me why it made you feel all crazy, we can talk about it. But until then, tell me about you."

Amber told him that she was born in Atlanta, and she had a brother who died at birth and her little brother, his twin, Xavier was six. She also told him that her stepdad, Zaharias, had died too so that is why her mom moved to New York and about Zacharias' son, who had committed suicide earlier that year. Amber went on to tell him all about her grandma that lived with them in Atlanta but moved out when the bad thing happened that she did not want to talk about. Her grandmother, Anne Marie Baptiste, had died last year and that is why she went back to Atlanta for those two weeks. She explained it all to Morales. She told him that there is a period of her life that she just cannot remember from when she was between the ages of ten and eleven. The doctors could not understand why either.

Morales and Amber sent text messages back and forth to each other for several hours before she realized that it was three in the morning, and she had to get up at six to take Xavier to his bus stop and then walk to her own. She texted him goodnight, and he responded with a sleepy-faced emoji. She laughed and went to the bathroom to brush her teeth to go to bed. When she returned to her room, there was a note underneath the door that led to the outside. When she opened it, it said "I really enjoyed our texts. Smell the paper." When she smelled it, it smelt just like him. She held it close to her chest and fell backwards on her bed.

A year had passed and Amber and Morales were going great. Nothing could have prepared Amber for all the excitement that she had with him since that first encounter. Morales would pick her up for lunch in his Magnum and Amber was the talk of the school. She was known as the "good girl gone bad." Everyone was shocked that the cool yet quiet athlete scholar was taking a risk and dating a grown man—and in the open to top it all. But no one said anything out of the ordinary. It kind of made her more popular than she was before. He treated her so kind. He took her out when her mom thought she was with Cheyanne. He bought her things and her mom thought she was just spending the money she made working as a babysitter or from the social security checks she got from her deceased grandmother and stepfather. Life was good, especially her sex life.

Morales took his time with Amber. He did not rush her into her first time. But one day, Amber just got sick of the kissing and holding hands and occasional fondling. She wanted more, but it was a

if Morales was the one holding out on her. One day, Amber was sleeping in her bed, and there came a knock on her window. It was Morales. She locked her bedroom door in the house and opened the side door that led to the outside and let him in. He looked her deep in her eyes as he pulled her close to him. "I was dreaming of you. Are you ready?" he asked as he pressed her close to him and she could feel on her body how ready he was. She swallowed hard and looked back up at him, "Yes. I think that I am. I know that I am," she said nervous as ever. Morales laid Amber down on her bed and began to kiss her and remove her pajamas. Morales kissed Amber over every inch of her body, and once he reached her private area and kept kissing, Amber almost exploded.

Morales placed his hand gently on her mouth and proceeded to continue to kiss her. He stopped and looked at Amber as he removed his own clothes. He opened a condom wrapper and placed it on his own private part. He whispered in her ear, "This may hurt. It may hurt a lot but I will go slow and be gentle as possible." Amber nodded as he placed himself inside of her. Amber let a soft yelp but slowly came into her zone of pleasure and pain. Morales did just as he said he would, and Amber was pleased beyond measure at what was happening. The emotions that she was feeling was something that she knew would not be able to describe in words. Morales slowly rocked his hips back and forth until Amber shook in what she thought might be a seizure or a heart attack. Morales had a smirk on his face by this time. "You came. It's ok. That is supposed to happen." Within the next 20 minutes, so

did Morales. This was the first of many experiences that Amber and Morales would have.

After that first time, Amber seemed to not get enough. These two were like rabbits. They did it everywhere and anytime they got the chance to. If her mom was at work or church, he came to her house. It was easy to distract her brother because he was always engulfed in his video games or outside on his bike. Xavier was oblivious to the freaked-out nature of what his sister was embarking upon. Amber had officially been turned into a nympho by her older lover. But no one knew. That summer before her senior year was her own personal sex-cation, and Cheyanne thought that it was too funny. "Girl you have turned into Madonna and Dennis Rodman!" Cheyanne explained to Amber while they were at one of their famous sleepovers. "Is he coming through tonight?" she asked as she painted Amber's toenails. "No, he has this new job working for the State of New York, so he is sleeping. He needs to. I am so tired, and we need to shop for the school year. I cannot wait. I wonder what this year has in store for us?" Amber says as she blows on her toes.

The summer finally passed, and the long weekend was finally over. Amber and Cheyanne returned to school. It is always crazy coming back after a long weekend especially since school had just started back. The kids always wondered why school just did not start after Labor Day. Why come back a week before only to be off again. Oh, well, this is senior year anyways. There was so much to look forward to. Amber was excited about Homecoming, Senior Week, Senior Trip, and Senior Prom. The only thing that made these things

less exciting is her newly found relationship with Morales. She could not take him to any of these things because of his age.

What would she do? She sat on the bus as these things ran marathons in her head. She had to think quickly because she did not want to miss out on these things that she has waited since freshman year to participate in because she wanted to date an older guy. Maybe she should date a guy at the school and not say anything to Morales about it. She sat straight up in her seat and looked over at Cheyanne and exclaimed: "I know what I am going to do Cheyanne. If they think I am a good girl gone bad, just wait until they find out that not only am I dating and banging an older guy, but also I am going to date the one guy that everyone wants: Benjamin!" Cheyanne could only just stare at Amber in disbelief until she did not even realize her mouth was wide open and her gum had fallen out. "You are really turning into a slut or a pure doggone *thot*. I cannot believe it. Lord, help us all," Cheyanne says finally closing her mouth.

Chapter 4

Amber was talking so fast when they got off the bus; Cheyanne did not know what to do. She just walked with her and nodded. She was not able to get a word in edgewise. When Amber finally stopped talking, Cheyanne stopped walking. "Girl I thought that you were going to have an asthma attack or something the way that you were talking without doggone breathing. Ugh. I think you've given me a blasted migraine," Cheyanne said as she rubbed her temples. "Look, you know I am down for you hooking up as much as possible and safe as possible before we are off to college, but dang girl. You want to juggle two men at one time? That is going to be a task for you since this is one of the first real relationships that you have been in."

"I want to enjoy my senior year just like every other girl that is in the twelfth grade; and unfortunately, the man that I love graduated from this same school when I was in the fifth grade. So, I guess I am going to have to be Benjamin's old lady. It isn't like he won't be dating someone else anyways. You and I both know he is a lady's man, and it is not like I am going to do it with him because I have Morales for that," says Amber holding her straps of her book bag tight and looking like a little kid in a candy store. "Well, okay, there he is. Go ahead and talk to him," Cheyanne says pointing across the courtyard in Benjamin's direction. He was with all the other athletes in the middle of the courtyard, talking smack as usual about all his "other" extracurricular activities he has had.

Amber walked over to Benjamin with a new air of confidence that Cheyanne had never seen before. She thought that Amber was getting a little cocky since she started dating Morales. She liked this new-found self-assurance. Amber seemed bolder and daring since she started dating Morales. Cheyanne felt as if Amber's morale was at an all-time high. This made Cheyanne quite proud to be her best friend. She had always told Amber that she needed more tenacity. Amber was high spirited when it came to her athletics and education; but when it came to real-world situations such as relationships, she was quite monotonous.

"Hey there, Mr. Benjamin. How are you this morning?" says Amber with such swagger in her voice and body language. Benjamin looked down at her in disbelief. "Really, you want to have a conversation with me? Um, well, I guess I am okay," Benjamin said feeling very jarred by the sheer presence of Amber. He had always wanted to talk to Amber; but even though they were acquaintances, he never tried to date her because he knew that she was aware of his bad boy status. He was into breaking hearts and collecting panties; but he liked Amber and no one, not even Amber, knew this. "Boy, stop playing. You know we are friends!" Amber exclaimed touching the small part of his arm. Benjamin almost toppled over, so he sat down casually as if he was not stupefied by this little interaction with Amber. "Yeah, I know. So, what's good Left Twix!" Benjamin said jokingly. He always called Cheyanne and Amber Left and Right Twix because when you saw one, you saw the other. He used to call them Kit Kats in middle school, but they grew a whole lot, he told them.

Amber sat next to Benjamin and leaned in close to him. The smell of her perfume and the touch of her skin to his made Benjamin's heart flutter. He kept his cool because his boys were looking at him oddly as if they could tell that Amber had him in the palm of her hand. "Are you still dating Rayland? Or is it another hoochie?" Amber asked as she drew invisible circles on his kneecap. "No, I am single," Benjamin says almost not being able to get the words out of his mouth. "Ok, so here is the thing. I have heard that we would be the best power couple of the senior class. I like you and can tell that you may like me, too. So, let's just say we hook up. I will let everyone think you asked me out just now, and we get to know each other better and see how it goes. The whole school cannot be wrong, can they?" Amber spits these words out at Benjamin a mile a minute; and he stares at her while trying to understand that he was just asked out by the girl of his dreams; and he is speechless. "Benjamin are you still with me?" Amber questions him while she leans over even further. She was so close he could smell the toothpaste and peppermint on her breath.

He stared down at her lips that were perfectly covered with shiny pink lip gloss. He licked his lips and took a deep breath in as he mouthed the word "yes." "I think it could work out babygirl. So, watch this," Benjamin says as he wraps her in his arms and plants a big delicious kiss on her mouth. At first she was shocked as she was being kissed but as it continued, she totally melted in to his arms. Benjamin slowly releases her from his grasp. She opened her eyes and looked around, and the whole school has come to a halt. Every person within eye distance of them was stiff as boards and stared in their general

direction. Cheyanne screamed and ran towards them. "So I guess you guys are a couple, huh?" asks Dillon, Benjamin's best friend. "I guess they are!" says Cheyanne while she elbows him in his side.

The whole school was in a whirlwind about time the second bell rang to switch classes. Everyone now knew that Benjamin and Amber were now a couple. It was inevitable some thought. Then, you had those jealous girls who were wondering why it was not them who Benjamin had chosen. Some of these girls had done some of the most unthinkable things to get his attention. They have sent him naked pictures on his cellphone. They have pulled him behind the portables and let him cop a feel on their breasts or behinds. Some even offered to take him shopping or to let him do some very dirty things to them—that's because they wanted to be the so-called Queen of the school. They wanted to be the All-Star athlete's girlfriend so that they could get the respect that Rayland used to get. But ever since their big breakup, Rayland became one of the "normal" people.

She was just that. Even though Rayland was also a cheerleader and in the choir, they did not give her the cool points that she had when she was with Benjamin. Rayland knew that she had to find a way to break these two up. She was determined to make Amber's reign as queen short-lived. How dare Amber try to take her spot? Everyone knew that Rayland and Benjamin would be back together in no time, just like always. Amber had overstepped her boundaries this time. It was bad enough, in Rayland's opinion, that Amber was already popular in her own right. Amber was head cheerleader, lead in the choir, one of the fastest track runners in the district, and was a straight-A student.

Now, this chicken head has stolen the man of Rayland's dream. She was not going to let Amber ruin her plan to be Benjamin's woman forever. It was on and Rayland was ready for war.

Nothing could ruin this day for Amber. She had her school boyfriend now so she could just act like a normal teenager now. She loved it. As the days went on, her and Benjamin grew close. They talked on the phone all the time and hung out after school when there weren't any games or practices. Morales was always so tired from work that he barely noticed that Amber was not as attentive as before. Amber and Benjamin became practically inseparable, and Morales basically had no clue. Well, at least that's what Amber thought. What she did not know was that Rayland had found out about Morales and was plotting to find a way to get the information to him about Amber stepping out.

Rayland followed Benjamin to Amber's house one day when he was dropping her off from a date at the mall. Benjamin and Amber were looking for something to wear to the Homecoming Dance that was coming up in October. They both knew that they were most definitely going to be king and queen for the senior class at Homecoming, so they had to look the part. Rayland took a sharp turn and slammed her car directly in front of Benjamin's cherry red Camaro. He almost tore the back off her little Nissan Sentra. Good thing he was paying attention or he would have knocked her into oblivion. Benjamin jumps out of his car while Amber slides out of the passenger side smiling nonchalantly because she has a feeling what's about to g

down. She throws her hair into a quick messy bun with the hair tie she always had on her wrist and straps up her black Air Force Ones.

"Your mind must be completely gone because why in the holy hell did you just whip your car in front of mine like that?" yells Benjamin waving his hands all over the place. "Nah baby, she must be cruising for a bruising because if she would have smashed the ride, I would have smashed her face. Don't let it fool you little baby. I am from the 'A' don't forget that, and we don't play about our man or their ride," Amber says as she approaches Rayland. "I am not scared of you female. Did you tell Benny about your *old* man that you had before him and still with?" Rayland yells and points towards Morales' house. "Did you happen to tell good old Benny here that you are banging your neighbor and that is why you are playing Mother Theresa with him?" Rayland says.

Before Rayland could say another word, Amber slaps the spit literally out of her mouth, and they start fighting. Amber is quite brutal for a girl her size. Rayland is at least five foot nine and one hundred and fifty-eight pounds, but Amber uses her small frame and quick feet to dodge every other swing Rayland throws and almost knocks her completely out. Benjamin is so stunned at what is transpiring that he almost doesn't stop it until he notices that it is drawing a crowd. Benjamin springs into action and separates the ladies before they rip each other's hair out and clothes off. "As turned on I am by all this fighting over little me, I need for you to get your ass out of my girlfriend's yard before that Haitian mother of hers comes out and lay some voodoo smack down on you. Rayland, we are done, and there is

nothing you can say to change that!" Benjamin says as he slings her as gently as he can in the direction of her car. "Peace out chick!" Amber says throwing up the deuces and walks confidently back to Benjamin's car to retrieve her belongings and her bags from their mall trip.

Benjamin walks her to the front door, gives her a kiss, and waits until she goes inside. He goes to his car and feels as if someone is watching him. He looks up and meets eyes with a man he had never seen before. It was Morales, but he did not know that. Morales had pulled up during the fight and watched it the whole time and was about to come over until he heard what Benjamin said to Rayland. He was in utter shock and wondered how could Amber betray him.

Chapter 5

Amber took a shower and got dressed and ran all the way to Cheyanne's house. This was just too juicy to tell her over the phone. She almost ran Cheyanne's mom over trying to get in the house. "Sorry ma, I have something urgent to talk to CheChe about!" Amber yelled back as she ran to Cheyanne's room. Priscilla just laughed as she left the house. She was used to getting almost knocked over by Amber and Cheyanne since they became friends in the sixth grade. Priscilla Louis thought that Amber was a good influence on Cheyanne. If she only knew what mischief these two got into and were about to cause after tonight.

"That witch almost killed us in his car and then we scrapped. I am good, but you should have seen her face when Benny said that it was over between them. That is when I almost died girl," Amber says as she flops down next to Cheyanne on her king-sized bed. Cheyanne laughs, "I wish I would have gone with you to your house like you asked me to. I just needed to charge my phone because dude was supposed to call me." She was talking about Benjamin's best homie, Dillon. Dillon Parks was like that quirky little sidekick that every superhero has. He was the Robin to Benjamin's Batman. He was the Booboo to Benjamin's Yogi Bear. He was the running back on the football team. Benjamin was the quarterback. They meshed so well on the field. It was just fluid.

"Wait, so you really going to actually be faithful and date one guy? And you are telling me the that it is going to be Dillon?" Ambers

says with her hand on heart. She pretends to faint and falls over on Cheyanne's bed. Cheyanne hits her with one of her pillows. "Yes, yes, I am and what is the problem with that? It is senior year. You are not the only one who can make a change in their life that is so drastic. Geesh Amber," Cheyanne scoffs at Amber. "I am sorry. I can see that you are serious about this. So, I guess I will be taking your black book and locking it away!" Amber says jumping up from the bed and opening the drawer of the desk. "I did not say all of that honey," Cheyanne says as she jumps up laughing and slams the drawer back closed. "One thing at a time. It is like the steps the rehab people take. What is it seven steps?" Cheyanne says as they both laugh and fall back on the bed. "What are you going to do about Morales though?" Cheyanne asked Amber. Amber sits up and just stares off into space. What is she going to do?

Morales could not believe what he had seen. He could not understand why and how Amber could have done this to him. She got whatever she asked for and more. She never went without. He did whatever she asked him to do even if he did not want to. He loved Amber. He thought she loved him. They had exchanged "I love you" so many times that he lost count. But now, he sees that someone else has gotten her attention. He was not about to lose her to some high school boy. He had to make sure that she was his no matter what; she belonged to him. Morales laughed as the plot to keep Amber his forever took a trip of completely sadistic ideas in his head that involve getting that pissed off young lady he had seen leaving as an intricate pawn in this new game of his.

The next day at school, the rumor mill was a buzz about how Amber embarrassed Rayland. Everyone knew about how she beat her up and how Benjamin completely rejected the idea of ever getting back with Rayland. What was also shocking to the whole school especially Benjamin and Amber was that Rayland was quite calm and friendly to everyone at school that day. She went around the school hanging her posters for Homecoming as if nothing had happened. Her best friend Bianca was a little eerie about the whole thing. "Are you sure that you are okay, Rayland?" asked Bianca with the sound of real concern in her voice "I am fine girl. We have to get these posters up before lunch remember?" Rayland said smiling and hanging up a poster. "I may not have the king, but I will for damn sure be Homecoming Queen for the senior class, and nothing is going to stand in the way of that!" She took another poster from Bianca and continued down the hall.

Homecoming was quickly approaching, and everyone was very excited. Amber and Cheyanne spent their time putting up posters for Amber to run for Homecoming Queen for the senior class also. They were unaware of anything else going on but Amber winning. Her only competition was Rayland, and Amber could not have cared less. She knew that she was a shoe in because first off, she was the girlfriend of the king and, secondly, who would not vote for her. Amber was too excited. She had Morales take her to the most expensive boutique to get a dress. She told him that she would be going with Cheyanne and some other girls. He even rented them a stretch Hummersine for the evening and rented them a suite for the night so they could have an after-party when Homecoming was over. You would think it was prom

the way that Morales was shelling out the dough for Amber. He told her it did not matter that he was not going to be there, if she was happy. She had second thoughts at first and felt bad that he could not go, but she loved the fact that he spent money on her. That was one of the reasons why she loved him.

Amber liked Benjamin, but she was in love with Morales. She liked how he treated her and how he never made her feel like she was a little girl trying to be a woman. Morales made her feel relevant in the world. He never made her do anything that made her feel uncomfortable, and he always was very attentive. He just had a problem with being jealous. This is what made her feel nervous because she was not sure what would happen if he found out about Benjamin. She was starting to like Benjamin. It was starting to not feel like an arrangement anymore. She was starting to have feelings and that made her more nervous and a little happier than ever.

What also had Amber quite bewildered was that Cheyanne stuck to her word. She was being dedicated to Dillon. She locked her little black book in a box that was being hidden by Amber at her house. Cheyanne deleted all the guys out of her iPhone 6s so that she could not call any of them if Dillon happens to get on her nerves. She was being the model almost girlfriend. Her and Dillon were taking it slow and not giving each other official "labels" until after Homecoming. They wanted to date each other and get to know each other before deciding if they were going to go official. This shocked the whole student body because even the freshman knew that Cheyanne was kind of a loose girl to say the least and Dillon was no

your typical monogamous fellow. These two people being taken off the market came as surprise to everyone especially their friends. They called their bluff literally every day, but they both stood their grounds. Amber was very proud of her friend. She was happy that she finally had a steady and stable relationship that was not based on sex.

The Homecoming game was three days away, and everyone was sitting attentively waiting in the last period. They were all so in a mood because the afternoon announcements were late coming on. Today was the day that Principal Dodson would announce who would represent the senior class at Homecoming and wear the official title as "Mr. and Miss Towson Catholic High." They were basically the king and queen of the Homecoming just like prom. Everyone had bad nerves just waiting. Even the teachers were in a panic because they knew that if the wrong names were called, then the classes would be in a disarray until the bell rang for dismissal. The announcement bell rang, and the televisions automatically turned on.

"Good afternoon Towson. This is your Principal, Mrs. Dodson. I have some very exciting news for you that I know that you are eagerly awaiting to hear. Only the senior class representation will be officially announced. The others will be placed on the school news wall."

Principal Dodson clears her throat and continues. "Okay here we go. The class of 2017 for Towson Catholic High will be represented by Benjamin Williams and Amber Hollingsworth!" You could hear an uproar in all the classes. Cheyanne and Amber were in their AP

American Government class and literally knocked each other over exchanging hugs and kisses on the cheeks. They were so excited and so was the rest of the school, except for Rayland and her small click of friends. There was a slow clap that came from the back of the class, and when Amber looked back, it was Rayland. She had stood up and was walking towards Amber. This was one of the only classes that they shared. Rayland got real close to Amber and leaned over and whispered in Amber's ear. "You may have won again, but it is not over bitch!" Rayland hisses as she brushes past Amber and Cheyanne and walks out of the class. The class dies in laughter and mumbling of crazy noises "Well, I guess she is mad or nah!" laughs Amber as she wipes her shoulder off and texts Benjamin. The dismissal bell rings, and the class continues to be just as hectic as they all leave to go home.

Amber and Cheyanne were laughing about what just happened in the class. While they were chatting, Benjamin and Dillon strolled up behind them. They had heard about the interaction with Rayland Benjamin was worried. "I am fine, Benny. That little mouse does not make me fret whatsoever. Je ne suis pas inquiet!" Amber says she walks towards the bus. "What did you say woman?" Benjamin says scratching his head. "You forget I am half Haitian, right? You need to learn French. I said, 'I am not worried,'" Amber laughs and gets on the bus and blows Benjamin a kiss. "You don't want to ride home with me after I lift weights?" Benjamin says flexing his muscles. "No, I want to go home and see if my mom is going to let me drive her Mercedes to the mall so I can get my nails done. Your queen has got to look good at the game and the dance," exclaims Amber as she waves goodbye and

pulls Cheyanne to the back of the bus. Cheyanne shrugs her shoulders and waves goodbye to Dillon while being dragged to the back of the bus. "I never get a word in between the both. and now we are speaking other languages?" Dillon says looking more confused than usual. Benjamin wraps his arm around his friend, and they turn to head towards the locker room to change so they could lift weights.

Amber was so excited when she woke up Friday morning. She had seen Morales the night before, and he was such the sweetest thing. He took her to the drive-in and had got her some Red Lobster takeout. Since they could not go places where folks would recognize her and know that he was not her brother, they usually went to the drive-in and ate takeout. She hadn't minded before and, since being Benjamin's girlfriend, did not care that much about that. When she was not with Morales, her, Benjamin, Dillon, and Cheyanne were on double dates. This was the time she could be footloose and fancy-free like most teenagers dating people their own age. She did not have to worry about hiding, and her mom was cool with Benjamin. Even her dad, Felton, had come down from Pittsburgh to meet him. It took a lot to impress these six feet seven, mocha brown, CIA agent, who did not like anyone near his only daughter.

Chapter 6

Felton Hollingsworth was much like Benjamin. He was the finest brother on the block when he met Amber's mom in College Park. They went to the same high school. Leslie and Felton both played basketball and grew up in the same neighborhood. Not only did he play ball, but Felton sold marijuana. He was not some nickel-and-dime brother either. He was selling it by the kilos. This excited Leslie. She was much like Amber when it came to boys, but worse. She did not talk to boys; she did not look at boys; she barely even knew how to act around boys.

This was because of Amber's grandmother, Anne Marie. She was a bible-toting, strong-willed, good old devout Haitian Catholic who had the fear of the Lord embedded in Leslie's head. All Leslie did growing up was go to school, extracurricular activities, and church at least five days a week. That is the main reason why she dated Felton secretly. He was an escape from her church world. They dated all senior year; but when her mother found out shortly after graduation she made sure she went to Bethune Cookman for Education since Felton decided to stay in Georgia and go to Georgia Southern to study Forensic accounting. Anne Marie tried to keep them apart, but when Leslie came home her sophomore year for Thanksgiving pregnant Anne Marie knew she had failed.

Felton and Leslie grew apart after being married for three years deciding that they married too young. Leslie went on to finish school and met an older gentleman named Zaharias. Zacharias was the

mailman that delivered mail where Leslie lived back home. When she had finished school, she moved back home to Atlanta to take care of her ailing mother who had had a mild stroke. She started working at the Dr. King Junior High in Atlanta as an English teacher. She wanted to be a college professor or maybe an editor at the international publishing company in Atlanta. She had a minor degree in journalism also. She dreamed of being a big-time editor at Anthem International Publishing, but she was awaiting responses back from her applications at the universities first. One day when she was coming home from work, she ran into Zacharias, literally. She almost hit him in his mail truck with her car.

That was all it took—just that one incident turned into a whirlwind romance. They went on several dates. Zacharias told her that he was recently divorced and had a son named Zacharias II. Zacharias II lived with his mom in Seattle, but he was fighting for custody of him. Leslie knew a lot about the law, so she decided to help him get custody of his son. She took him to get the paperwork to show that Zaharias' mother, Allison Pryor, was unfit. Allison smoked marijuana around him. She put locks on the cabinets, so he could not get anything to eat. He was only eleven years old, and he was deathly afraid of her. She would leave him in the house alone. When she was home, she verbally abused him. Allison was also a lesbian who always had multiple women in and out of the house. She, on occasions, would walk around the house naked with some of these ladies, while Zaharias II was home. He felt very uncomfortable around his own mother. It took almost six months, but Zacharias II finally was sent to his father

to live for good. Allison was placed in jail for 5 years for child abuse, child neglect, and child endangerment.

Zaharias was so elated that he finally had his son and Leslie was the reason. He knew then that he loved her more than life itself, and he had to marry her at once. They were on a trip with their new church home, Mount Hermon AME Church, and he asked her to marry him during the call to worship. The whole church was very happy for them, and Leslie could not be any happier. Amber was happy that she was getting not only a big brother but also a new dad to take care of them. What she did not know was that her life would be forever changed because of these nuptials.

Leslie and Zacharias married that following spring, and Anne Marie thought they just rushed into it. Anne Marie always asked a lot of questions when it came to Zacharias. She always told Leslie that the spirits did not speak well of him. Leslie blew it off as her mom's usual voodoo priestess babbling and ignored her. No matter what she said she went on with the wedding because she was pregnant, and no one knew but her and Zacharias. At least that is what she thought. Her mother knew because the spirits had told her. She in fact was practicing voodoo priestess, and she went to the spirits about the quick wedding and was told that Leslie was with child.

"So you think that you are smart, aye?" Anne Marie say walking around Leslie in circles as she spoke. Her voice was big, but she was small. Anne Marie was four foot eight but had hips on her that children could literally sit on. Leslie would not make eye contact with

her mother. She had a feeling that her mother knew she was pregnant but had refused to tell her until after she had gotten married. That was why she waited two weeks to visit with her after the honeymoon to tell her so it looked as if she had possibly gotten pregnant right before the wedding. In fact, Leslie was already four months pregnant. "Manman an, ki sa ou vle di?" Leslie says to Anne Marie speaking Creole. Whenever she was nervous, she spoke in her native tongue. "Do not get scared now, my love. It is too late," Anne Marie says shaking her head. "The spirits told me that you are with child and that you have been for a while. Four months?" Leslie dropped to her knees and wrapped her arms around her mother. "I am sorry mamma. Do not be angry with me. At least I am married, and he is a good man with a good legal job. Not like Amber's dad," Leslie says crying to her mother. "Get up. It is not I who you should be apologizing to. Make sure you give this baby to God when he is nine weeks old or he will be cursed. I warn you of this now before the spirits come to him in his sleep. But there is not just one baby in there. There are two, but only one will live. Leave my sight now. Do not return until you have gone to the priest to confess of this sin." Anne Marie scoffs at her daughter, leans over and kisses her three times on her forehead, and returns to her room. Leslie stands in complete amazement and fear and exits her mom's house as fast as she can to get to the church to do as she was told.

Leslie had a hard pregnancy, and unfortunately, she miscarried nine weeks after her conversation with her mom. She did not talk to her for a while after that. Amber still walked to her house afterschool and spent weekends there but her parents would not speak to Anne

Marie. Anne Marie was still claiming to have dreams about twins, but she called Leslie and tried to warn her but she would not listen. Anne Marie was telling Leslie that it was not her who was having the twins but Amber. She said the spirits came to her in her sleep, and she had visions of two babies being squeezed by a black snake. One lived and one died. She felt that she needed to warn her about her husband and Amber. Leslie would not listen. She was so sick of her mother's ranting, and she stopped letting Amber go to her mother's house.

Amber was going through her own frustrations. She did not know what was going on with her grandmother and her mom because no one ever told her anything. She was always told to stay in a child's place and that grown-up business was not her business. So, she did not know that her grandmother knew exactly what was happening between her and her stepfather. No one knew that within two years of him marrying Leslie that Zaharias started molesting Amber. No one knew that not only was he molesting her, but also her stepbrother Zaharias II. No one could have possibly known that the sweet freckled-faced mixed little boy was making Amber do unexplainable things to him when their parents would go to bed.

Zaharias II came into Amber's room at night. This was before her stepfather started in on her. It was her stepbrother who started touching her before his dad did. One night, when their parents were at a church concert, Zaharias II came into Amber's room with nothing but a towel on.

had been accused of impregnating a young girl there, but the girl was undocumented so the family kept it quiet. Zacharias II stared down at Amber as he continued to masturbate onto her private area. She continuously cried thinking that would make him stop. "The more you cry, the harder I get. Have you ever seen anything as big as this on anyone?" Zacharias II asked as he rubbed his penis on her stomach. He began to thrust his penis between her exposed breasts. "I am going to let your hands go and if you move I swear you will die tonight!" Zaharias says as he releases her hands and tries to place his penis back between her breasts.

Chapter 7

"Muffin! Come back here. I cannot stand this dog," Amber yelled at her dead stepbrother's dog. Since his suicide, Amber had taken care of the Pomeranian. It was his mother's dog, but when he died, she could not bear to take him back to Seattle with her. Amber finally caught up with the dog and waved her finger in his face. She put him back on the ground and grabbed his leash. As she took him for his walk, she pondered as to why she did not have any memories of anything from the time Zacharias II was found dead in his room up until the time they moved after her stepfather's funeral. Things were very hazy for her for that whole year, but she did remember other things that sent chills down her spine.

Zacharias II was relentless. He never passed up a chance to get his hands on Amber. There was never a moment that he would not try to have his way with her. The only thing that kept him away from her was his father. Zaharias had his own plans in mind for Amber. He just used to watch her every time she would walk by. He would find reasons to touch her. Amber never thought of him doing anything to her at first because he was such an attentive father figure. Zaharias loved giving hugs; but lately, Amber took notice that his hugs got longer; and it felt as if he was rubbing himself against her like his son would sometimes do. She just thought that she was thinking too much into it because of what his son was doing to her on an almost everyday basis.

One day, everyone was gone from the house and Amber had stayed home from school because of cramps. She had not had her period yet, but her mom thought it may be coming soon, and this might be the day. She let her stay home and was going to come and check on her. They did not stay far from the school. Zaharias, unbeknownst to Amber, volunteered to come home on his mail truck and check on her so Leslie would not have to. Amber was lying in her bed sleeping when she suddenly could feel weight on top of her. When she opened her eyes, her stepfather, Zacharias, was lying on top of her. She thought he was just joking like he sometimes does when he comes in and jumps on her bed and tickles her.

"Get up you crazy man!" Amber says jokingly and smacks Zacharias on the arm. But the look on his face was a look she had seen before, and when she looked at him, she soon realized that he only had on a t-shirt and his boxer-briefs. She began to tremble with fear. She knew this all too well. What scared her was that this was her mom's husband and the man who vowed on their wedding day to love her child as his own. Was this the love that he promised to show her?

"I have come to get what is due to me little girl. All that money I spend on you and you walk around here half naked teasing me all the time. You wrong for that, you know?" Zaharias says as he starts to undress. "Now you are going to let me do whatever I want to or else will leave you and your mom without a cent. And you going to have to go live back with your grandma. Now rent is due so open up. I am about to teach you what a girl supposed to do for the man who pay the bills." Amber is crying hysterically by now and wishing that he

mom would come home and see what he is doing and blow his brains out. She just lays there because she knows that she cannot get this man off her without him seriously hurting her. She does not want to be the reason why her mom must move back home. This man was two hundred and eighty-five pounds and five foot nine. He was much bigger than her.

Amber begins to squirm thinking that if she could just get from underneath him, she could run to her grandmother's house up the street. The more she moved, the more he pushed his weight back down on her. He slapped the side of her thigh. "Stop moving little girl. It will not hurt that bad." She was unsure of what he meant by the hurting part. He pinned her down on the bed and started kissing on her. She cried loud as she could, but he grabbed her face and stared at her with the look of a wild man. Her cry settled to a low moan because she was afraid of what he might do because when she turned her head away from him, she saw a small switchblade on her nightstand. She knew it belonged to him and was afraid of what he might do to her. She saw him use it before when they were fishing on the creek. He took his hand off her face and rubbed her small, almost not even there, breasts. The tears rolled down her face in utter silence.

He sat up off her body and slowly caressed every inch of her small frame. He removed her panties and rubbed his index finger against her exposed vagina. He licked his finger and tried to insert them into her; but because she was a virgin, it was too tight. This angered him for some reason. "Why are you not ready to pay me little girl?" he says and slaps her again on her other thigh this time. He held his

erection in his one hand and spread her legs with the other. He began to rub himself in a similar way as his son did when he attacked Amber the first time. He stared at her as he rubbed vigorously.

This made Amber very nervous because he got closer and closer to her as he rubbed himself. Suddenly, he forced himself inside of her with one swift stroke. She screamed as loud as she could as she felt a warm watery substance leave her body. She thought she was dying. He stroked three times as she screamed in pain and then stopped. "I do not want to hurt my baby so I am going to give you a little break for a minute. But I will be back. Go clean yourself up. I will tell your mom, you got your period," he says as he gets up and pushes her over to remove the blood-stained sheets from the bed.

Amber laid on her side for a minute and cried. She placed her hand between her legs and saw the blood leaving her body. She just wanted to die. She wondered what she had done to deserve this. Why was she being molested by the only two men in the house? Why did they feel the need to touch her? Now she was bleeding. She prayed for God to come and take her away, but He did not. She just got up and took a shower and made her bed as she was told. Her mom had called and spoke with Zacharias as he told her that he found Amber lying in her bed bleeding in her sleep. Leslie said she knew that she would probably get her period because of the bad cramps she was having and what to get her from the store.

"Amber are you alright, baby? Leslie asked her over the phone. Zacharias stared at Amber as she talked to her mom. She knew by h

look that she better kept the conversation short and sweet and to the point. "I am fine mamma. Just a little cramping and a lot of blood. Pops gave me a pad from your room until you get home because he says he isn't going to the store. He does not know what to get and all of that. I will just go when you get off or walk to grandma's house," Amber says not breaking eye contact with Zacharias. He nods his head in agreement and then takes the phone from Amber. He caresses her behind and pulls her close. "Yes, our baby is growing up. I will fix her some lunch and have her go lay down. Okay. Bye baby. Love you," Zaharias smiles at Amber and hangs up.

He takes his hand and grabs Amber's and rubs it on his exposed genitals. "Since you're all bloody now, I need you to help me finish what you started," he says as he rubs her hand up and down his hard penis. Amber begins to cry again as she complies with what she is told. He walks her slowly while she is doing it to the sofa and he sits. This continues for another five minutes until he finally climaxes. He takes her shirt and wipes himself off. "Throw that shirt in the laundry hamper and go lay down until I call you to eat. If you tell anyone what we do, I promise I will leave y'all and maybe you might end up missing. It all depends on you," Zaharias says and points his finger at Amber. Amber gets up and takes off her shirt and throws it in the hamper in her bathroom. She goes to her room and closes and locks her door. She lays on her bed and decides that she is going to tell someone she knows will help her. She will tell her grandma, Anne Marie. Amber knows that her nanna always had her back.

Amber was too afraid to tell her grandmother. The torture from her stepbrother and stepfather went on for another 2 months. It was around Christmas time, and she noticed that Zaharias II had not been in her room bothering her since Halloween almost. That was the last time. He realized that she had been with someone, and they had taken her virginity. He asked her who and she said she did not know what he was talking about, and he got mad and rammed a lollipop inside of her and left her room. That was the last time he ever tried to abuse her again. She was happy that at least one person gave up on attacking her. She just had to deal with her stepfather. Since that first penetration, he only did it again one more time. He found pleasure in her hand jobs and ejaculating on the outside of her vagina. He told her it was just too risky. That and her mother was pregnant, and he had to have sex with her because the pregnancy elevated her sexual hunger. This frustrated him because he only wanted her daughter. But Leslie did notice a shift in the household.

It was that Christmas when things began to change. Zaharias I was not himself. Anne Marie had been spending a lot of time around the house. She even slept over a few times. Amber thought it was just because her mom's pregnancy was proving to be quite difficult. Also Amber had been sick lately. It was early on in Leslie's pregnancy, but she was at risk due to her sickle cell anemia. She was only six weeks and she was having a bad time with the pregnancy. Anne Marie was thinking that a bad omen had fell upon the home, and she was then cooking and praying off evil spirits that she said is walking through the

home. Leslie, as usual, thought her mom was just a little crazy but liked that she was there taking care of everyone.

Anne Marie walked into Amber's room while she was on her laptop and suddenly fell to her knees. "What happened here child?" Anne Marie says holding her chest. "Who came in here and did these vile things?" she says as she spreads her arms and hands into the sir. "I see the affliction you are feeling, and it will be reckoned with I assure you!" Her grandmother sprang to her feet and grabbed a hold of Amber. "No one messes with my grandbaby. I will remove the person or persons from you, and you will no longer feel or know of the pain that they have caused," Anne Marie says as she rocks Amber back and forth in her arms. Then, she suddenly releases her from her grasp. She places her hand on Amber's stomach. She begins to cry. "A spawn. Oh no, this cannot be. You will never know that pain until God has blessed you with a husband." Anne Marie cries and bends and whispers into Amber's ear as she places her hand on her forehead and then her belly.

Amber stares at her grandmother and just cries and nods as this is all happening. Too much is going on now for her to even respond. By this time, her mother enters the room because she hears Anne Marie beginning to wail in Creole. "Oh Bondye. Sèvi ak fòs ponyèt ou a detwi lènmi yo ki te vyole pitit fi m 'yo. Se pou mechan yo gen pou wete nan men fòm terèstr yo ak jete nan lanfè," her grandmother wailed—which translates into: "Oh God. Use Your mighty hand to destroy the enemies who have violated my granddaughter. Let the wicked be taken away from their earthly form and cast into hell."

"Mother, why are you in here crying and casting curses upon people about Amber? What has happened? Amber what is wrong?" Leslie says shaking and trembling when she sees the pain on her daughter's face. Anne Marie spins around looking as if she is possessed, "The ones who have touched her will be extinguished, and she will not even remember what has happened." Anne Marie turned back to Amber and mumbled something under her breath and Amber faints. Her grandmother scoops her up from the floor and lays her on her bed. She takes a vial with an oil in it out of her brassier and applies to her forehead while still mumbling this whole time.

Chapter 8

Leslie paces back and forth. She knows not to ask her mother anymore questions, but she is afraid of why she has done this. She suspects her husband or stepson is one or both of whom her mother speaks. "This will all soon be done!" Anne Marie says as she turns and leaves the room and grabs Leslie by the hand. As she leads Leslie to the kitchen, she continues to say her inner prayers. They get to the pantry where her mother takes out some herbs and mashes them and grinds in them into the mashed potatoes Leslie was making for dinner.

"Only feed these to the boy. I have something else planned for the man," Anne Marie says. "A month after the son is gone. I will begin work on the man. But the demon seed must not know where he comes from. So we will send her back to our country until he comes full term; and when you give birth to your boy, he will not live. Your grandson will be his replacement. He is to never know who is his mother for this will be his curse. She will not remember this until she turns 21. Then, she will have the gift of sight as I do now."

Leslie starts to cry but knows that she must not deny her mother this. She heard of old tales of people being killed for wrong doings by the voodoo from her country, but she had not believed it. But now she hopes and prays more than ever that this will work. No one hurts her baby, and now she must carry this baby that won't live anyways. She will get a child in return, but it will be her grandson and not her own baby. How could they do this to her innocent baby? She is only in fifth grade. What does she know about being a mommy? She

won't be though. These thoughts became overwhelmed with the feeling of wanting to inflict the most pain she could on them both.

Anne Marie made dinner for the family and ensured that only Zacharias II ate the mashed potatoes. Since his father only liked rice and beans mainly, it was easy not for him to eat them. Leslie told Zacharias that Amber was not feeling too well, so she was sleeping after taking one of her sickle cell medications. She had it just like her mom anyways, so the lie fit in well with the usual occurrences of crises she frequently had. Everyone sat quietly during dinner. No one said anything. Leslie spoke up just to break the silence, so the two evil men would not know that they were caught. The conversation was quite dry but at least, it was not dead silence any longer. Zacharias II stood up suddenly.

"I am feeling like a migraine is coming on. I had a bad day since about an hour ago. Seems like my world is just spinning out of control. I got kicked off the basketball team. The girl I liked turned out to be a transgender, and I failed two exams. I hate life right now," he says as he slams his napkin down on the table and ran upstairs. "Let him go," Zacharias says as he places his hand on top of Leslie's. "He is a man. He can handle it. Wait until he gets in ninth grade," he scoffs and continues to eat. It took all the will power Leslie had in here and a look of death on her mother's face not to stab Zacharias with the steak knife on the table.

Zacharias got up from the table and left his plate and proceeded to the living room to watch television. Leslie and he

mother cleared off the dining room table and took the dishes to the kitchen. When they got inside of the kitchen, Leslie nearly collapses and her mother catches her and helps her to the kitchenette table. "How long before this happens? How long do I have to bare this pain mother?" Leslie says as she places her hands on her stomach and looks up at her. "If I say the prayer right, you may have both babies, your son and hers. But I do not know. These babies were breed by an evil man. Pray my child. It may turn out better and faster than you think. But the boy must die first before we can go home to Haiti to prepare for the big one's demise," Anne Marie says brushing her hand on her daughter's head and turning to clean the kitchen. "Rest my baby. It will begin tonight."

Screams of a man's utter panic filled the air of the house about midnight. Footsteps were heard through the house running towards the sound of the scream. It was Zacharias. He found Zacharias II in his room slumped over and unresponsive in his bean bag chair by the window. There was a heroin filled syringe on the floor with a makeshift tourniquet wrapped around his lifeless arm. There was foam coming from his mouth and no pulse. Next to his body was a note. The note said: "I can no longer deal with the pain that I have caused myself and others. I have been using for about a year now, and it will be my escape from this world. I am sorry. Goodbye."

Zacharias called 911, and soon there were flashing lights of an ambulance and the police outside. The EMTs could not find a pulse and stated that he had been dead for at least an hour. The family wept as they took the body out. Amber was still sleeping during all of this,

and her mom could not go and wake her up. Even though she kne
that she would be upset about his death when she found out, she d
not want her to see the pleasure she had taken in knowing that this w
just the beginning of her mother's wrath. It would soon be h
husband's turn to meet his maker, and she hoped her mother wou
allow her the pleasure of speaking to the spirits on this one.

The following week, Amber went with her mother ar
stepfather to prepare for the funeral. Amber was still dazed about ho
she could have missed or forgotten all the things that her mother to
her about Zacharias killing himself. She could not understand why h
would do such a thing. She only could remember good things abo
him. They used to play hide and seek and freeze tag and just goof o
all the time. Oh, if she only knew what was hiding in the depths of h
brain and in the pits of her stomach. Amber also was noticing that sh
was gaining a little weight, but she blew it off with getting her perio
and getting older. Her mother and grandmother told her that sh
would lose the weight when she went on her 6-month vacation
Haiti.

The funeral was very nice. The basketball team came
Zacharias II's funeral dressed in white t-shirts with his face ar
number on it and their basketball sweatpants. They looked very nice
they helped the pallbearers walk his casket into First Presbyteri
Church. Zacharias and his son did not worship at the Catholic Chur
that Amber and her mother attended with her grandmother, so the
had his funeral there. No one knew the cause of the boy's death. H
father had a friend at the police station that ensured that the news d

not find out the cause and made sure that no one in the hospital would disclose it either. The funeral lasted about an hour with brief speeches from distant relatives and people from the school that Zacharias II attended. His mother said a few words alongside Zacharias but had to be carried out a short while after. She could no longer be consoled.

Leslie felt only slightly bad. She did not care that he was dead, but she felt a mother's pain. She wished that his mother knew the pain that not only he inflicted but also her ex-husband on her child. She shook off those feelings of guilt and walked alongside her soon-to-be-dead also husband in the funeral procession. They got into the limo and went to the graveside. There were dozens of balloons released, and the graveside ceremony lasted for fifteen minutes. Everyone said their final goodbyes and went back to the church where the repast was being held by the members of the church.

Anne Marie, Leslie, and Amber left the repast early and blamed it on migraines that Anne Marie were having. When Amber got home, she went in her room to pack as instructed to by her grandmother. She was feeling quite odd but did not think anything of it. She did think that it was strange for her to be going to Haiti for six months. She would miss a lot in fifth grade, but her mom was taking leave as a teacher and would home school her. She did not mind. She just figured it was best for the family. What was seemingly different is that her stepfather was not going. He always went with them to vacation trips but not this time.

Four days after the funeral, Amber, her grandmother, and mother said goodbye to her stepfather. He looked like a kid in the candy store as he watched them board the plane. He was planning on having all types of women over since his wife would be gone for six months. He wanted to have that young white chick over that keeps on flashing him her breasts at work when they are picking up their mailbags in the mornings. He decided that he was just going to give her what she has been asking for—the big black mamba. He laughed at the thought of plowing that sweet young white behind from the back. She did text him that she likes it rough. He planned on doing just that.

Anne Marie and the girls arrived in Haiti within hours of boarding their plane in Atlanta. They were going to be staying with Leslie's uncle, Mauricio, in Pétionville in Port-au-Prince. It is one of the richest communities in Haiti. It is like the suburbs in Atlanta. Amber was so excited because she had not been there since she was five. They were picked up by Anne Marie's brother Mauricio in his Hummer along with ten bodyguards in three Mercedes-Benz. "Alo fanmi an Byenveni tounen nan Ayiti," Mauricio says to his family as he runs to hug them all. "I am so happy to see you. When I got your message about the situation, I sent for you posthaste!" He looks down at Amber. "Oh my baby!" he hugs her in his arms and then places his hand on her head and mumbles just the same as Anne Marie did the day Zacharias II died. Amber faints. "She won't remember or feel thing," he says as he carries her to the Hummer and the guards get the luggage.

Three months pass and Amber has been in a comatose state since they arrived in Haiti. She is now six months pregnant and no one back home knows it and neither does she. She is fed with feeding tubes, and the baby is monitored by the machines set up in one of Mauricio's many villas. Leslie calls home every other day to check on Zacharias; and the last time she spoke with him, he said that he had the flu and just could not shake it. He was complaining of losing his hair in clumps and breaking out of rashes on his back and feet. He went to several doctors, and they keep changing the diagnosis. He says that he thinks he is sick because she is gone with his daughter and she needs to come home. She just tells him that she will be home soon and that she is dealing with the family business in Haiti.

The day that Amber was officially eight months pregnant, Anne Marie decides that it is time for the plan to come almost full circle. Mauricio, Anne Marie, Leslie, and two more elderly gentlemen join them in the basement of the main house of Mauricio's. They sit in a circle. There are candles lit and several bibles are on tables in the room. There is a hairbrush with Amber's hair in it and a shirt that belongs to Zacharias along with his picture. They place these items in the middle of the circle and begin to chant scriptures from the various bibles. "A solemn prayer is what we need to God to tell Him of the hurt that this man has caused, and then, His will shall be done!" Mauricio says and paces the floor and prays as the others continue to read the scriptures. After the scriptures are finished being read, they all begin to cry and pray and the whole basement is filled with loud wailing and moaning and then the candles went out.

Twenty minutes later, Anne Marie, Leslie, and Amber board a private plane along with Mauricio back to the States. Amber is still asleep, and she is being taken care of by a medical attendant from Haiti. They land in Atlanta about three hours later, and Leslie receives a call as they are getting off the plane. "Hello. Is this the wife of Zacharias Pryor?" asks the voice on the other end. "Yes, it is. Who is this?" asks Leslie. "This is Officer Kingston of the Atlanta Police Department. Your husband was found dead in front of your house, ma'am. We need you to come down to the hospital to identify the body. Your neighbor said you were in Haiti." Leslie staggers back and almost faints. "I just landed. I will be right there. Is he at Grady?" "Yes ma'am. He is," Officer Kingston says. "I will be there in thirty minutes," Leslie says and hangs up. "It is finished. Take her home. Take the back roads and go in through the back door so no one sees that she is with child. We will have a home birth tonight for the both of us after I identify his body, and this will be the end of my poor baby being trapped in her mind and body," Leslie says as she gets into the black Lincoln. The luggage is unloaded from the plane; and Amber and the rest of the family gets into the black SUV and head to the home while Leslie goes to Grady Memorial to identify Zaharias' body.

Chapter 9

Amber was taking a shower, getting ready to go get her hair done for the Homecoming game. She rubbed soap on her stomach and caressed the scar that ran along it right underneath her navel. She did not have the slightest idea how she got this scar. Her mom told her that she had fallen when they were in Haiti when she was in the fifth grade. She did not remember; but if her mom did, that was all that mattered to her. Amber was so ready to have a great time at the first official event as a senior. She knew that this was just the beginning of such a great last year in high school. She jumped out of the shower and looked at herself in the mirror. "Damn, I look really good!" she laughed as she checked out her naked body from every angle.

Cheyanne arrived at Amber's house in a rental car. It was a yellow drop-top Porsche, and she looked real nice in it when she pulled up. The neighbors stopped and stared at her when she arrived. She honked the horn and got out. Cheyanne leaned on the car like she was a multimillionaire's daughter. The sunlight glistened on her chocolate skin, and her lip gloss glimmered on her beautiful pouty lips. Cheyanne was so proud of her melanin, and it showed that day. "Girl, you must think your poop smells like roses?" Amber yelled as she ran outside to the car. "Yup and my pee smells like White Diamonds," she said as she laughed and hugged her friend.

"Are you ready for the turn-up of this year? Because prom will be the turn-up for next year!" Cheyanne says as she gets into the car. "Yes, I am and I cannot wait until it is time for prom. This

Homecoming is a practice run for the ultimate turn-up of the senior year," Amber says as she slides her slender body into the hardback sports seat of the Porsche. "Girl this seat is like butter to my behind. I have to make sure that I make bank as a neurosurgeon because I need about three or four of these bad babies in my garage," she laughed and slapped her friend on the hip as they pulled off. They drove off not knowing that they were being watched.

Cheyanne and Amber gossiped some more while getting their hair done by Miss Exclusive. Miss Exclusive was the hottest hairstylist in the game. She was not bad looking either. She had a Coca-Cola bottle shape and the prettiest white teeth you have ever seen. The teenagers loved her because she was hood smart but a business woman and they could talk to her about anything. She had been doing the girl's hair since they were in middle school. She had a great bond with Amber because Amber's mom and Miss Exclusive played basketball in high school together, were college roommates, and basically were best friends. Miss Exclusive was like family to Amber.

Miss Exclusive owned the biggest beauty shop in Upstate New York. It had a spa in it along with a beauty bar where any woman could get their nails and makeup done. Amber being her godchild, so to speak, made it great for her to get her services done for half the price which extended to her best friend Cheyanne. So, they got the all inclusive treatment for Homecoming. This day of beauty before the game is something that they both needed after the stress of midterms and just being a teenager in their eyes.

"So, how are you two ladies doing today? I am loving the styles you picked. You are going to kill them at the dance!" Miss Exclusive exclaimed as she walked over to the girls while they were under the dryer. They both smiled and extended their arms towards her for hugs. "We are fine ma. How are you doing? How is my brother Mr. Money Bags?" Amber said and winked her eye at her godmother. She laughed, "Brenton is fine, child. I am going to be a grandmother again. His wife is pregnant, and this time it is twin girls. I am glad because they already have three boys. She spits out babies like a baseball fan eating sunflower seeds at a baseball game." The girls laughed at her. Brenton was Miss Exclusive's youngest child who was a running back for the San Francisco 49ers. He was the ultimate athlete, and he spoiled his mother. He was the one who bought her the salon and spa when he got his NFL contract along with a brand-new house. Her daughter Tanya played for a basketball team in Europe but was wrapped up in her own life and experiencing it as a single woman. Miss Exclusive barely heard from her. Her oldest son, Marshall, was a college coach for Xavier University's football team. He got injured when he was in the NFL and had to retire, but he always visited his mom with his wife and two sons. Miss exclusive was a great mother and everyone knew it.

After the two girls had their day at the spa, they went to the school to get dressed for the Homecoming game. They had to dress to cheer, but Amber did not perform because she did not want to get sweaty as she had to walk for Homecoming Court during halftime. Amber was so excited and could not wait to see Benjamin in his suit. She laughed when she thought about how she had not even spoken to

Morales in almost a week, and he had not made one attempt to see or talk to her. At this point and time, she did not know if she even cared anymore. She enjoyed being a teenager and not hiding her relationship from anybody. She still loved Morales, but she did not think that she was "in love" with him anymore. She was in love with Benjamin.

The game was going good. They were beating their rival, Winston Marsh High School, 32-7 when the clock hit triple zero at the end of the second quarter. Amber already had left the field to get ready for the presentation of crowns. On her way, back to the field, she ran into Morales. He grabbed her by the arm and yanked her around so that their eyes locked on each other. "I need to talk to you right now!" he grimaced as he spoke to her through his teeth. She snatched her arm away from him and fixed her beautiful light pink chiffon dress. She brushed her hair out of her eye and off her shoulder and shot him a look of death. "I do not know if you lost what mind you have, but if you ever grab me like that again, you will draw back a nub," Amber said as she turned around and continued back to the field. "I know about you and that tall football player, and I am done with your trifling young ass!" Morales spit out those harsh words as he flicked her off. His cousin, Duncan, was with him. He went to the school with Amber and the gang, and he had been giving information to Morales along with Rayland. Rayland and Duncan were dating now, and they both conspired against Amber and her crew.

"Ask me do I care old man. I was going to break up with you nicely, but since you and your poop-faced cousin want trouble, now you've got it. If you say one more thing to me, I will tell my dad you

forced yourself on me. Now that is trifling, isn't it?" Amber said and flicked Morales back off. By then, Benjamin was coming out of the boy's locker room and shot Morales a death stare. Morales puffed his chest out to make himself look bigger, and Amber whispered into his ear. She had somewhat told Benjamin about who Morales was but left out when and how she got with him. Benjamin waved his hand in a motion that would be read as "go away" in Morales' direction and took Amber into his arms, kissed her, and walked her towards the sound of the already screaming crowd in the stadium. Duncan had to hold Morales back. "Dude, he would eat you alive," Duncan said as he pushed Morales towards the exit.

Amber smiled as she waved and walked onto the field with Benjamin. She was glad that the chapter of her life with Morales was finally closed. It was too much work trying to keep up with him, hide Benjamin from him, and then still have a normal teenager's life. She kind of felt bad about how it went down, but Morales had brought it on himself. He was the one trying to be all macho. Now look what it got him. He is alone and was embarrassed in front of his people. That is strictly his problem. She could not wait to tell Cheyanne about what happened. But she did not have to because someone had seen what went down, and it was already on Instagram and Snapchat. That is why the crowd went extra wild when they walked onto the field. They had become a social media hit. The feed had hit two thousand views in under two minutes since it had been posted and shared twice as many times. It was crazy. Cheyanne was on the sidelines with the other cheerleaders going crazy. "Girl, you and the old man are on social

media!" Cheyanne yelled at Amber from the sidelines and pointing at her cellphone.

Amber covered her mouth in disbelief but continued to smile and wave as they got on the back of the golf cart for the parade around the track. Amber pulled her phone from her small handbag once she was settled on the back of the cart and noticed she had so many tags and posts on her phone. She cleared them and turned her phone off. She was just happy that her mom only used Facebook as social media. Her mom would just die if she found out about Morales. Her only worry was if her dad, Felton, would find out. He was ex-CIA for Christ's sake. She thought that he would have access to all her social media even if she did not want him to. She decided that, just in case, she would call him later tonight and let him know what happened, so he would be her backup if her mom would happen to find out or if he happened to use his CIA skills to consider her social media.

Amber and the crew had such a great time at the Homecoming Dance. With a new-found release from the shackles and burden of having to deal with hiding her relationship with Morales, Amber partied like it was her last day on Earth. She danced the night away. Cheyanne even noticed that her best friend's light shined brighter than it has for a long time. She was happy for her. "She is really coming into her own," Cheyanne thought to herself. Cheyanne ran over to her friend and hugged her, and they danced with each other. They laughed and laughed until, when Amber turned around, she saw Rayland and Benjamin leaving the dancehall holding hands through the back door.

Chapter 10

Amber loosed her hands from Cheyanne's and sprinted across the dance floor, between tables, and out the same door she saw Benjamin and Rayland go through. What she saw surprised her completely. Rayland and Benjamin were arguing. She stood to the side that they would not see her. She listened as hard as she could.

"Rayland, why can't you just leave me alone? Does Duncan know you are out here?" Benjamin asked frustrated with Rayland constantly harassing him. "Do you know about the dude that she is seen on social media arguing with?" Rayland asks trying to sound concerned. "I do know, Rayland. Is there anything else you want to tell me or ask me? I have a woman and a dance to get back to!" Benjamin says as he turns and walks back in the direction of the dancehall. He looks up and sees Amber standing and waiting for him. She smiles. He does, too. Rayland looks at them both with tears in her eyes. "Yeah. do Benjamin. I am pregnant and it's yours," Rayland yells and storms out of the exit doors to the parking lot.

"Crazy chick just said she is what?" Amber frantically says as she points towards the direction Rayland walked away and braces herself against the wall. "She is just saying that to ruin our night. She knows that if she was pregnant, then I would take care of it," Benjamin says as he grabs a hold of Amber at her waist. "Let's go back inside and pretend that neither she nor the old head ever existed and have a good time." He kisses Amber on her forehead and hugs her. Amber hugs

him back with a little bit of hesitation and distrust in the pit of her stomach.

After the dance, an Uber picked the kids up, and they went to Amber's house for the coed sleepover her mom was having for them. She separated the living room so that the boys would not be able to get to the side where the girls were without walking through the kitchen by her mom's room and her seeing them. They had a great time in the media room watching movies in the theater seats, and they stayed up until five Sunday morning. The whole crew slept until one in the afternoon when they were awakened by the smell of eggs, bacon, toast, and the works. Leslie was in the kitchen with her boys making breakfast for the crew. Amber and her friends took showers, got dressed, and devoured the brunch Leslie had made.

Leslie followed the teenagers to the rental car place in her Mercedes truck so that they could return their cars they used for Homecoming. Once they were returned, they all got into the truck and would not stop talking about the events that occurred Friday night and Saturday night. She looked in the back and was happy to see how Amber had grown into a lovely young lady. She almost teared up at the thought of Amber knowing the horror that she had been through when she was in the fifth grade.

She wondered if she remembered any parts of it. Leslie shuddered at the thought of her being with her friends and suddenly having a memory come back to her. She would bring it up in a conversation later that evening. She would see what she remembered

and what she was shady on. She knows that her mother, Ann Marie, said that Amber would not have any memories triggered until she was 21 and her gift of sight would be happening until then, but she was very skeptical about that timeframe. Amber has always been intuitive, and she was very afraid that a memory or something would trigger it before time. She did not want those floodgates to open. She had to ensure that it would not affect her going off to school. Nothing would get in the way of Leslie making sure her child would never know that one of her "twins" was not her brother but her son.

Leslie arrived to the hospital to identify Zacharias' body. She was quite happy that he was dead. He was such a bastard. He was abusive and an adulterer. Then, to find out that he sexually abused her daughter was the straw that broke the camel's back. She felt as if she did not protect her daughter from this evil she brought into her house. But she would not have known. He was good at hiding his flaws when they met. No wonder his wife divorced him and let him take his good for-nothing son with him. Like father, like son truly applied to these idiots. But now, her daughter would be safe and she gets two more beautiful children out of it. She just had to put her game face on for these police. There was no forensic test in this world that could detect that good old voodoo that her mom did oh so well. She laughed but changed her composure as soon as she turned the corner and almost knocked over the sheriff.

"Are you the wife of Zacharias?" Sheriff Rosewood asked Leslie. "Yes, I am," she said as she made her voice quiver. "Okay, ma'am. I am sorry to say that we think that this is your husband and he passed away right in your front yard. We just need you to identify the body," he said as he guided her towards the glass window of the morgue. He knocked on the glass, and the coroner pulled the curtain back. On the slab laid the man who had molested her daughter for years. Leslie's eyes filled with tears and she cried out. The sheriff thought she was crying out from grief and despair, but these were tears of joy and peace that she received from seeing that monster lying there cold and hard as steel. The sheriff embraced her and kept her balanced as he could.

"I am sorry for your loss. I am moving from Atlanta to New York in a few weeks after I finish the paperwork on your husband's case. If you need someone to talk to, here is my card. I am also a grief counselor," Sheriff Rosewood said while handing Leslie his card and smiling with compassion in his eyes. Through her tears she looked at him and realized that he was one of the finest specimens of man she had seen in a while. She hurriedly took his card and stuffed it into her Gucci saddlebag and took a handkerchief from the pocket of her fleece Prada pants. "I sure will. Just after I deliver these boys of mine," she said quickly and patting her very pregnant belly. I was supposed to come home and have a water birth with my husband next week, but I guess he will miss the birth of his sons," she said wiping her eyes. "I can be there if you want!" the sheriff said. "No, no, no," Leslie said rather quickly and shocking Sheriff Rosewood. "That is a nice gesture,

but we have just met. I will call you once I have my boys and get my husband's affairs in order. You have been quite nice. Where can I pick up his belongings? I must go home and break the news to my family," Leslie said and started towards the elevator. Sheriff Rosewood guided her through the process and wished her well as he walked her to her chauffeured car and she left the hospital.

Leslie rushed into the house and slammed the door. Her mother and family already had the birthing ritual set up and were awaiting her arrival. She went to her room, showered, and dressed herself in a long white robe-looking garment. She wrapped her long well-cared for auburn hair in a white hijab-type head covering. She said a prayer and then went back out to the front room. On a mat next to a huge kiddie pool filled with water was Amber. She was dressed the same way her mother was. She looked so angelic and in peace lying there except for a huge belly. It looked so out of place on the body of such a small child. It made Leslie angry, but she continued to pray so that the evil thoughts would not affect the baby.

Leslie's uncle, Mauricio, placed Amber in the first pool while Leslie steeped into the second one. She sat down and looked over at her daughter. She placed her hand in Amber's and closed her eyes. The family began singing in Haitian Creole and quoting Bible scriptures. The room was filled with the smell of fay ave maria, mombin fwar basilisk, and Florida water. The leaf bath will allow the babies to come into the world free of negativity and blessed. The prayers and the songs that filled the room caused Leslie to feel the contractions. She wailed and moaned in utter pain and despair. She cried as she looked over an

saw Amber's tiny frame jerk in pain that she could not feel. The family members laid their hands on her and the jerking stopped. The priestess took a sharp knife and began praying over it while running it through the flames of three candles. One candle was white, one was a pale yellow, and the other a deep blue. She was praying the prayer of healing and safe delivery in Creole. Just then, Amber's body went limp. Leslie's baby began to crown. The priestess took the knife and walked over to Amber. The other people in the room crowded around Leslie and her daughter, and the chants got louder. Leslie passed out from the pain. The priestess took the knife and sliced into Amber's abdomen. She reached into Amber's belly, cut into the amniotic sac, and removed Amber's baby.

Once the baby was removed, another woman grabbed the baby and took it into another room. You could hear the baby crying from the front room, and this is when Leslie came to. The woman brought Amber's baby to Leslie, and she cried as she held him. A family member was with Amber and stitching her up as Leslie pushed three times and the other baby boy was born. He was also taken to another room; and when she heard him cry out, Leslie was relieved. The same woman brought her son back to her.

Anne Marie walked over to Leslie and placed her hands on her. She began to pray vigorously and looked to be in a trance. Then, she looked deep into Leslie's eyes. "You are the cause of this child's despair because you did not heed my warning not to marry this man. You are charged to ensure the well-being of Amber and these boys. Your punishment will be that you will never be able to bare anymore

children because you did not protect the one you had." Leslie began to cry. "Hush those foolish tears. It is of your own fault. If you do not take care of these boys equally, yours will be cursed and hers will flourish. Heed my words this time mon ami," Anne Marie said as all of the candles went out at once.

Chapter 11

With Homecoming behind her, Amber was busy hitting the books so she could maintain her 5.0 GPA. All Amber had on her mind now was track and schoolwork. Finals and holiday break were just weeks away. She was determined to make sure that she would not risk the opportunity to get scholarships from the best schools. January, was it. This was when all the schools would start sending out their offer letters. She was already cleared by the NCAA clearinghouse to accept offers so it was smooth sailing for her.

Amber could not understand one thing though. She kept having headaches and bad dreams. She kept having dreams about twin baby boys and her grandmother. The dreams were driving her crazy and causing her trouble sleeping at night, and she hated that. She did not want to worry her mother because she was busy trying to get one of her author's books published and printed before Christmas rolled around. It was November 30, and it was another two and a half weeks before Christmas vacation. It was crunch time for them both. Thanksgiving came and went like nobody's business, but it was quiet at the Pryor household, even though Leslie started dating the cop that she met when Zacharias' body was identified back in Atlanta. They ran into each other at a coffee shop in downtown Manhattan when she was meeting with a client who wanted to have a manuscript published.

Sheriff Rosewood's full name is Nicholai Rosewood. He now works as a lead detective for the NYPD at the First precinct downtown. She laughed when thought about how she seemed to have

a thing for men in law enforcement. She vowed to never date a mailman again. Nicholai was treating her very well. She decided to just date him and not get too serious because the last man she loved and trusted molested her daughter and impregnated her. He seemed quite genuine in his feelings for her. Her wall was still up though. They have dated for almost six months, and they had not slept together nor had he met Amber. He spent time with her and the boys, but she always made excuses why Amber was either never around when he was or that she does on her own thing. Nicholai thought it was odd but did not complain. He did not have any kids of his own; but at forty-two years of age, he did not want any, so dating a woman who already had kids and did not want anymore was right up his alley.

Nicholai was a looker to boot being such a nice guy. He was six foot seven and two hundred and eighty pounds. He was a dark chocolate man with a bald head and beautiful lips. He was originally from Turks and Caicos and moved to the United States when he was fifteen years old with his single mother and six siblings. He was the oldest and only male. So, he had a passion for treating women right because he grew up taking care of his sisters. He knew what a woman needed and when she needed it. He had a sense of when to give woman space or when she needed for him to be there for her. This is what made him good for Leslie. He had bad relationships in the past because women always took advantage of his kind soul. But with Leslie, he did not have that worry whatsoever. He just could not break down that wall. He told her one night at dinner that he would spend his whole life trying to make her his. Leslie held him to that.

Leslie decided that with Christmas around the corner, she would finally let Amber and Nicholai be in the same room. Leslie wanted Nicholai to feel like he was part of the family since he made it clear that he was not going anywhere. She wanted to see how true that was. If he tried anything or if she even catches a whiff of him looking at her very well-developed daughter, he would suffer the same fate as her deceased husband and stepson. Anne Marie would do the same if she was still alive. Oh, how Leslie missed her mother. She was always there for her when she needed her. Anne Marie was the pillar of their home, and now, she had been gone for almost a year.

Anne Marie was a Haitian immigrant who came to Atlanta with her husband who worked for the government. Aristae Baptiste was a government agent who retired due to being wounded during a failed bombing at the embassy. He moved his wife and then-newborn Leslie to Atlanta where he worked at the courthouse as a linguist. Anne Marie worked as a cafeteria manager at the local elementary school. Leslie was the only child because Anne Marie did not want any of her children to be born a US citizen. She felt obligated to keep the Haitian blood running strong and through her daughter. That is why she was so upset when Leslie grew up and got pregnant by Felton who was Jamaican–American. But she loved her Amber with every breath she took until her last. Even on her deathbed, she reminded Leslie of the promise that she made. Therefore, Leslie kept Amber and her boys as safe as she could.

A few weeks had passed and Amber and her mother were decorating the house for Christmas. They waited until the last minute.

They were not big celebrators of Christmas because of Anne Marie and her beliefs. But Leslie decided that she was going all out and let Xavier, Isaiah, and Amber have a real Christmas. Amber was too excited. Amber could not remember Christmas between the time she was in fifth grade until she was in the eighth grade. Those memories of anything seemed vague and far and few in between. She shrugged it off as she listened to her mother sing Christmas carols and she joined in. The boys danced around and just got in their way. Amber rushed them away from the glass decorations and told them to put on their winter gear and go outside and play in the light snow that had fallen overnight.

Suddenly, Cheyanne comes rushing in. "Turn on the news. Oh my God. It is Rayland," she yelled as she turned on the flat-screen TV in their front room. There was live coverage of a house two streets over. That is where Rayland lives. There was police tape surrounding the house. They were bringing out a body bag on a stretcher. The news reporter was saying something about what happened, but all Amber could do was stare at the screen. "Amber snap out of it girl. Rayland killed herself. Her mother found her hanging in the garage with the car running," Cheyanne said trying to shake Amber into reality. "She left note saying that she was tired of being ignored by those she loved. Girl do you think she killed herself because she was pregnant by Benjamin?" Cheyanne said and stepped back away from Amber.

Leslie snapped around and looked at Amber and Cheyanne. "What did you say?" Leslie asked and slowly sat down on her white leather recliner. "Rayland told Benjamin the night of Homecoming that she was pregnant by him. No one believed her. She told Duncan, an

he said he did not want to be no other dude's baby's daddy and broke up with her. Her mom threatened to put her out if she did not have an abortion. Benjamin would not talk to her. So, baby girl hung herself." Cheyanne spit the words out a mile a minute. Amber slid herself down on the floor in a pile of decorations. All she could do was cry. She was not crying because Benjamin got another girl pregnant because from what she heard, it happened before they hooked. She was crying because no one would listen to Rayland, and she felt like she played a role in it. "I need to call Benjamin!" Amber said as she picked up her iPhone 6s Plus off the end table.

Before she could even dial the number, her phone began to ring; it was Morales. "Hello?" she said stiffly. "I bet you like a piece of crap knowing that your boyfriend's ex killed herself because of y'all! You ruined everyone's lives!" Morales yelled at Amber and then hung up. Amber looked around and started to cry again. Leslie tried to console her, but she got up and ran to her room and slammed her door. Cheyanne followed behind her. She told Cheyanne what Morales had said as she was shaking and trying to call Benjamin. Cheyanne took the phone and called Benjamin for Amber. "Girl, forget his old crybaby behind. He is just bitter like an old divorced woman with 12 cats," Cheyanne said jokingly trying to cut the tension in the room. Leslie stood at the door and eavesdropped. She wanted to be sure her daughter was okay.

"Benjamin, do you know about Rayland?" Cheyanne asked before he could even answer the phone good. "Yeah man, damn. I told my old girl what happened and she slapped the spit out of me. I

thought she was lying. I feel horrible. Where is my baby? How is Amber?" he asked with such hurt in his voice. "She is here balling like a baby. You need to get here ASAP!" Cheyanne ordered and hung up. She threw the phone on the bed. "Just like that bitch. She wanted to ruin everyone's Christmas and make it all about her. She should have just taken an ultrasound and gave it to him," Cheyanne said to Amber while beginning to cry herself.

"Why are you crying?" Amber said sniffling and wiping her nose with her hand. She got up and used some hand sanitizer Cheyanne looked up at Amber with such hurt in her eyes. "What is wrong Cheyanne? This is not about Rayland, is it?" Amber asked as she sat down next to Cheyanne. "No, it is not about her. It is about me," Cheyanne paused and took a deep breath. "You know my uncle that I have no dealings with because I just do not like him, right? Well, he came over last month after I left your house Homecoming weekend. My mom was gone and he was drunk. She usually just lets him sleep in the spare bedroom. Well, when I was helping him to the back room, he grabbed me," Cheyanne stopped and looked around as if she was looking for an answer somewhere in the walls.

"He forced me in the room and ripped my clothes off. I tried to fight him Amber I swear, but he is so much bigger than me. He raped me Amber, and I took a pregnancy test last week because my period did not come. I was pregnant Amber. I told my mom and she told me not to tell. She took me to have an abortion. I just could not have his baby, Amber!" Cheyanne started to cry hysterically and fell into Amber's arms. Leslie came in and held them both as they all cried

together. "It's okay baby. Your secret is safe with us," Leslie said as she squeezed both girls. "This family has more secrets than you can even imagine. But do not worry. Momma Leslie has a cure for all evil men!" Amber sat up and looked at her mom. She wondered what that meant.

Chapter 12

Amber was still reeling from what Cheyanne said. It is crazy that she did not notice her gaining a little weight. Cheyanne was what they called "slim thick." She basically had all her weight in all the right places. But she could not get over how her own uncle had sexually assaulted her and even how Cheyanne's mother just took her to have an abortion all nonchalantly. Amber was almost in tears thinking about her best friend. It hurt her so bad to even think about having such a procedure done at their age. Amber just tried to shake the feelings off as she continued wrapping presents. She decided to take a break and to check on Cheyanne. She was asleep in the guest room at her house. Cheyanne had not been herself all week since she told Amber and Leslie about what happened to her.

Amber peeked in on her and Cheyanne was crying again in her sleep. Amber walked over to the bed, and rubbed Cheyanne on her back. Cheyanne jumped up out of her sleep and almost knocked Amber out of the bed. Amber grabbed Cheyanne with both hands and made her look at her. Cheyanne breathed a sigh of relief and laid herself back down. Amber covered her with the blanket and continued to rub her head and back. Cheyanne slowly drifted back to sleep. Amber hummed a sweet melody until Cheyanne began to snore. She smiled down at Cheyanne, kissed her on her cheek, and left her to sleep alone in the room. She closed the room door just slightly and stole a glance at her one more time before going back to what she was doing.

Amber called Benjamin on the phone because she wanted to take her mind off what was going on. She cried to him about how her friend had been hurt by someone she loved. He tried to ease her pain with kind words. There was nothing that could contain the hate and fury she felt for the man that hurt her friend. She told Benjamin that she had to make a call. Cheyanne came in as she was looking in the nightstand for her phonebook. Long-distance numbers to Haiti were not stored in her new iPhone 6s since she transferred from her Samsung Galaxy. Cheyanne plopped down and laid her head on the bundle of bears on Amber's daybed. Amber found her phonebook and dialed the number of her mother's uncle. She had not seen Uncle Mauricio since her grandmother's funeral last year. They took her grandmother's body back to Haiti after she passed away in Atlanta.

"Bonswa," Uncle Mauricio said happily as he answered his phone. He was quite the character. He dressed rather flamboyantly. He was always the life of the party back in Haiti and especially when he used to visit them in Atlanta. Mauricio did not consider himself a homosexual. He tended to use the phrase "experimental lover." He felt that he would make love to whoever loved him whether it was a male or female. But Mauricio was very feared in Haiti because even though his lifestyle did not depict it, he was a devout voodoo priest, and people came to him when they wanted to have dreams interpreted or problems solved.

"Bon aswè Tonton Mauricio. Sa a se Amber," Amber said as she sat back down on the bed near Cheyanne. "Well, long time no hear from darling. As you would say, what's good?" Mauricio said as he

took a sip of his wine and walked out to the balcony of his chateau in Cap-Haïtien. He loved the smell of the water coming off the beach. Amber kept adjusting the way she was sitting. She was very nervous about what she was going to ask her uncle. "I need a favor Tonton. I need you to get rid of someone for me," Amber asked as she started to bite her nails. "Stop biting your nails young lady. Why would you call and ask me these things? Is something wrong?" Mauricio asked as he sat his glass down.

This was a conversation that was oh so familiar to him. He remembered having this same conversation with her mother and grandmother years ago. He wondered what happened to cause this to come about again. "Someone has hurt my friend uncle, and they must pay. He has ruined her body and her mother made her get rid of the evidence. I understand why her mother did what she did, but her uncle is a bastard that must pay for his crimes!" Amber began to stand up and look at her friend who was now in tears and staring back at her in astonishment and in agreement. "I can be there in two days' time. I need you to not speak of this to anyone. Your friend must remain silent also. We will discuss this in person. Do you understand me?" Mauricio said as he hastily went back inside to contact his private chartered plane. Amber nodded as if he could he see her before she realized she was doing it. "Yes, I understand!"

Two days had passed and Cheyanne and Amber barely spoke at all to anyone except each other. They never spoke of the conversation with Mauricio and Amber. They went about their everyday routine as nothing ever was said or happened. It was like they watched a scary

movie and made a pact not to ever watch it again. Cheyanne and Amber were running up to the house from getting off the bus and ran right into Mauricio's chauffeured car. They looked at each other and simultaneously had chills run down their spines. They knew that this was going to be a long night. They ran inside of the house quickly and dropped their book bags at the door. Mauricio was sitting on the leather couch with his usual glass of red wine eating popcorn with Leslie.

Amber stopped in her tracks. "Mom, what are you doing home?" Amber asked her mom because she is never home when she got out of school. It was the last day of school for the holiday break. "Mauricio called me and said that he needed to see you. He said you need him, but he will not tell me for what. So, here he is and here you are. Now what?" Leslie asked as she went into the kitchen. Mauricio smiled slyly and shook his finger at his niece lovingly. "She was always so nosey. Don't mind her. Let us go to your room and talk there." Mauricio laughs and grabs both girls under their arms and strolls ever so gracefully down the hallway. He enters the room with the girls. Their faces are still in shock and disbelief as Mauricio drops his six-foot-nine, two-hundred-and-twenty-three-pound stretchy frame on the bean bag chair in the corner of Amber's room.

Amber quickly spits out everything that happened to Cheyanne. Cheyanne nods in approval ever so often but does not say a word. Mauricio listens attentively until Amber finally stops speaking. The room is quiet for almost two minutes. "So my love, all I need is something from your home that has hair or sweat on it. That is all. No

worries, okay. You will not even remember this conversation," Mauricio says as he gets up and mumbles a familiar prayer that Amber swears she heard before but cannot remember where. He walks up to Cheyanne, hugs her, and then places his hand on her forehead. She collapses in his arms and he places her on the bed. "'Now it is up to you to get what I need because she will not remember. But I will make everything better for her just like I did for you, mon ami," says Mauricio as he leaves the room.

Amber stands in the middle of her room looking very confused. She wonders what he meant by that. She does not know anything about him fixing anything for her. She never asked him for anything. Nothing has ever happened to her that she would need to be fixed. She started to undress and put on her running clothes. She wanted to go running in the freshly fallen snow to take her mind of what was going on; but as she took off her clothes, she brushed against the scar she had on her lower belly. Then, a thought popped into her head. She still does not know how she got that scar while she was in Haiti. Was this what Mauricio was speaking about? Did someone hurt her or did she hurt herself? She finished getting dressed and ran to the kitchen. "Mom, what happened to me in Haiti? What did Uncle have to fix for me?" Amber yelled looking at them both while they were sitting at the kitchen table. They both look at each other and neither one say a thing.

The silence that was in the kitchen was unbearable. No one moved. No one said a thing. It was as if a television was placed on mute. The whole world seemed to stop. Amber just stared at them

waiting for an answer, and they stared back at her not saying one word. She paced back and forth awaiting someone to either speak or leave. But nothing happened at all. She picked up a glass off the counter and threw it on the floor. "Are you alive in there? Speak people!" Amber yelled again as she picked up another glass and held it in midair. Her mother jumped up and grabbed the glass from her. Leslie began to cry and started to speak in Haitian Creole. Amber tried to pull away but Leslie had a good grip on her. Leslie continued to speak, but her words were muffled by Amber's skull cap she was wearing to go outside in. "My love, you were touched inappropriately by your stepfather and his son, and we made the problem go away. Now sleep. You won't remember a thing either," Mauricio said as Amber collapsed just as Cheyanne did in the room.

Chapter 13

Christmas was great for the Pryor family. Mauricio stayed over until after the New Year. Cheyanne still had not gone home before Christmas came. Her mother was happy to see her when she did stop by to get some things. She completely understood why Cheyanne stayed away so long, and their holiday went off without a hitch. Cheyanne's uncle had not been seen for weeks. There was word on the street that he had gotten one of the Italian mob's daughter pregnant and they placed a hit out for him. Amber knew that meant what Mauricio did had somehow worked or God was just on their side. Karma is a bitch however it played out.

Amber finally met her mom's boyfriend. Nicholai seemed cool. She especially liked how he purchased such great gifts for her mom and her brothers. She liked the Pandora bracelet that she received from him. She told her mom how nice he was and that he might just be a keeper. Nicholai was the first guy that her mom ever dated since her stepfather passed away. She was happy that her mother finally found someone that made her happy. Leslie deserved to be happy after losing her mom, husband, and stepson in such a short period. Amber believed that her mother was a very strong woman and that is what she loved so much about her. She hoped that she would be a great mom like her when she had children.

Months passed and it was almost time for the final field trip as a senior in high school, Grad Bash. She was so excited that she and her friends will be going to Islands of Adventure in Orlando. It was nice

for a change to be going with people her age instead of folks from the church or her family. Cheyanne and Amber had matching Nautica outfits and purchased a new pair of Jordan's with the money that they got from their weekend jobs at Aeropostale at the mall.

Cheyanne had done well not remembering what happened and so did Amber with what happened to her in Haiti. Neither one of them remembered a thing from that day that Mauricio came to Amber's home. They both had no clue how Leslie had stolen away in the middle of the night and snuck into Cheyanne's bedroom window. She left her bedroom window often at night so that her boyfriend, Dillon, could sneak in and spend the night. They also never knew that Mauricio and Leslie used the brush and panties that they found in her room to receive a vision of what happened to her. They saw that tragic day that her innocence was truly taken. It was all too much for Mauricio and the prayer he prayed to the spirits was such a strong one that he slept for nearly two days afterwards. Leslie had to finish the deed by going undercover and seeing the bastard uncle.

Leslie told Cheyanne's dad, Oscar, that she needed for him and his brother-in-law to move some items for her from her home office to their lawn for a garage sale she was having. He obliged. They came over and she flirted incessantly with the uncle. He took to her like a fat kid and slice of chocolate cake. Oscar just thought she was being extra friendly and paid it not too much attention. He excused himself to use the restroom and left the two alone for a moment. Leslie offered the brother in law a drink since they had moved all the furniture. He accepted the mixed drink that she made at the bar that was in her

garage-turned rec room. As he drank his cocktail, Leslie uttered a few words and rubbed her hands across his arm. He smiled and suddenly his smile turned into a grimace. Leslie whispered in his ear: "For all you have done to her, that much will be done to you three times over again!" He grabbed his chest and fell to the floor.

Leslie screamed and Oscar came running out of the house "What happened? What is wrong? Bro, I am going to call for help," Oscar says as he takes his cellphone out and dials 911. Leslie goes back over to the uncle and kneels as if she is going to give him aid and looks at him with a sneaky smile. She mouths "This is only the beginning" and then turns him on his back. "He just started to grab his chest and fell out of the chair while he was sipping on his drink. I do not know what caused it. He was fine," Leslie said shakily. Moments later, the ambulance arrived. They helped him to get stable and took him to the hospital. Oscar rode with him. The hospital told Oscar and the uncle's sister, Priscilla, that he had a massive heart attack and was lucky to be alive. He had a major blockage in his heart and was in surgery at that moment.

Priscilla was very upset. She walked away from her husband and pulled one of the officers to the side. She felt that she needed to tell them what happened to her daughter. She believed that this was sign from God, and she feared that He would soon seek justice for Cheyanne through her next. Oscar just thought she went over to let them know her brother's personal information. She began to tell the officer what her brother had done to her daughter and she almost broke down. The officer happened to be the lead detective that was

engaged to Leslie—Nicholai. Nicholai was extremely shocked to know that Cheyanne's uncle was a pedophile, but it made sense because she was always at Leslie's house. He took the information that Priscilla gave him and hugged her deeply. "I will place him under arrest if he makes it out of surgery, but I need to verify this information with your daughter. Do you think that she will speak to me?"

Priscilla did not know if she would. She had not seen her in a while. She only comes home to drop off dirty clothes and to get more before going back to Amber's house. She shook her head in disbelief. "I will speak with the D.A. to see if we could move forward without her testimony since she had the abortion. We can get DNA proof from the unborn fetus and you to show that they are related. Again, I am so sorry for what has happened, but I know that you feel more relieved to have gotten that off your chest." Nicholai patted her on her shoulder and left the hospital. Priscilla had so many thoughts in her head right at that moment. She felt horrible for praying for death to visit her brother as he lay on the operating table.

The surgeons came out and said that it was touch and go, but he had made it through the surgery. There was still a risk of him not making it through because of the major blockage in his heart that caused the heart attack. Priscilla stood and listened to the surgeon with such a blank stare that the doctor did not know if she even understood what he had just said to her. Oscar acknowledged what was said and took Priscilla over to the chairs to have a seat. "What's good, ma? Ya face look drawn. Did ya hear what da man say about bro? Just pray!" Oscar said in his heavy Bajan accent. She just nodded her head and

cried. If only he knew that his in-law who he was praying for to recover was the man that molested and impregnated his only daughter. She sat and held her husband and cried. Oscar sat with her and held her until she fell asleep in his arms. He sat with her for two hours until the doctors came out and said that he was in the cardiac care unit and was hooked up to several machines that were keeping him alive. This seemed to have angered Priscilla more, and she asked Oscar to take her home.

Two weeks passed and Priscilla's brother was still connected to the machines. There was a change in his prognosis. He was not on the ventilator and he was sitting up. He was still connected to a monitor for his heart. Lead Detective Rosewood went to the hospital when he was notified by the charge nurse that Priscilla's brother was awake. When he entered the room, it was as if he knew what was about to happen. His sister refused to come see him when he called her. Oscar had only been there a few times because Priscilla always found things for him to do instead of going to see her brother. Cheyanne had been there a few times with Leslie and Amber, and every time Leslie came his monitor would go off. So, the doctors told him that he should not have any visitors for a while until his condition was more stable.

"Mister Francois Augustine? I am Detective Nicholai Rosewood. May I come in?" Nicholai asked as he entered Priscilla's brother's room. He nodded and Nicholai moved closer to his hospital bed. "Sir, I am here about an incident that happened with you and your niece, Cheyanne Louis." Nicholai stated as he took his notepad out of his leather coat. "I am not saying anything without a lawyer present

Francois literally spit the words out of his mouth. "Well, sir that is fine because we have biological evidence that you not only molested your niece but the baby that she aborted was your child. You are under arrest for third-degree rape, aggravated assault, sexual abuse, and misconduct. I will now read you your rights," Nicholai said as he placed handcuffs on him in his hospital bed and began to read him his rights.

The other officers took a stand at the entry to his hospital room. Nicholai took out his phone and called Priscilla. "It is done. I hope this brings you peace." He hung up his phone and looked towards Francois. "You are an evil bastard, and I will make sure they get your ass in Morgantown. Oh, yeah, that is where you going because we know about the $5.5 million worth of cannabis and cocaine you have in that storage place in Yonkers. Oh, yeah, and we also know about that check fraud you got going with that chick you slept with. She was granted immunity, and she told us everything even about the judge who took that bribe from you when you got locked up for that insurance fraud." Francois sat up this time in disbelief with worry all over his face. His heart monitor went crazy and the nurses ran in as Detective Rosewood left the room laughing and opening his Blow Pop.

Chapter 14

The girls had a blast at Grad Bash. Rihanna and Drake were the headliners for the concert. Cheyanne and Amber enjoyed themselves so much with their boyfriends Dillon and Benjamin. It was the best time they had all year. Prom was next and that is all the students who were seniors could even think about—the final hoorah before graduation. This would be it. There was only the future to worry about. They all were looking forward to National Signing Day. They all would be signing their Letter of Intent next Wednesday in the gymnasium. They were so excited. They all received scholarships to the universities that they wanted to go to. Amber was the luckiest of the four because her school offered her not only an academic scholarship but also an athletic scholarship, which was very rare.

On the ride, back home from Florida to New York, the students were just jabbering away. The bus ride was twenty-one hours but they would be stopping in Maryland and sleeping before getting back on the road to New York. They did not care though. The bus ride was not an issue because no one seemed to be weary. They were all just full a joy and love. They talked about old times and things that they would encounter going to college. A lot of the seniors were happy because they would finally be seeing the world outside of New York and others were just happy to be getting away from their parents. Amber was happy because she knew that this meant Cheyanne would be far away from her uncle and this case.

Cheyanne still did not know what was going on with Francois. All she knew was that he was arrested at the hospital for messing with a little girl. She did not know that it was her. Because the abortion clinic had kept DNA of the unborn fetus, there was no need for her testify, which means that Mauricio and Leslie accomplished what they set out to do—protect her by any means necessary. Amber was also happy that she would be attending school with her best friend and continuing their reign as competition cheerleaders. She could not wait for cheer camp at her university.

The seniors finally arrived at Towson Catholic High and their parents and families met them with hugs and tears. While they were gone, something terrible had happened. Duncan, the boyfriend of now-deceased Rayland, had been in a terrible accident. He was drinking because he was depressed and was speeding on Hempstead Turnpike while visiting some family members in Nassau County and his car lost control and he crashed. He was ejected from the car and died on impact. He was not wearing his seat belt. All the smiles of the students turned into tears, moaning, and wailing. Grief counselors were already at the school waiting to talk to the now-grief-stricken students. How horrible was this that another classmate is gone too soon and to find out right after such an awesome trip?

After talking to the counselors, the seniors got into their respective vehicles and left. Amber and Cheyanne were greeted by Priscilla and Leslie once they had spoken with their counselors. They both hugged their mothers and went in Leslie's car. They got in and began to leave. There was an eerie silence in the car that Amber just

could not take. Amber began to say a prayer and Leslie pulled over and closed her eyes as Amber said a solemn prayer. When she finished Leslie looked at her in the rearview and nodded her head in agreement. She continued her way to her house. "I think I want to go to my home tonight. I think I want to be at home with my parents," Cheyanne said sitting up in the backseat and touching the shoulder of her mother. "That is fine with me, Cheyanne. I think it is time that you go back home. Everything is going to be alright from now on. Right Priscilla?" Leslie said as she looked over at Priscilla and winked her eye. Priscilla kind of jumped when Leslie did this. She was unsure of the wink, but she shook it off and nodded towards her daughter and kissed her hand. Cheyanne sat back in her seat and held Amber's hand all the way back to her house.

Amber did not talk to Cheyanne that much for the rest of the week. Cheyanne had been spending a lot of time with her family— especially in the wake of the trial of her uncle. She was not allowed to go to the trial. So, she spent her time studying for the last set of her finals and running every day. They saw each other at the track, but Amber knew the space was needed for Cheyanne to fully heal. Priscilla called Leslie every day with the updates of the trial, and so Amber knew what was going on. The final days of the trial were approaching and Amber was hoping that it would be over before Wednesday, which was National Signing Day. That would be a good way to end Spring Break. Then, it would be on to dress shopping for Senior Prom.

The following Monday came and the phone would not stop ringing. Amber ran to get it and it was Priscilla. "He is going away for

twenty-five years, Leslie!" Priscilla shouted before Amber could even say hello. "That is great to hear but this is Amber, ma," Amber says as she walks the phone to her mother in the kitchen. She handed the phone to her mom and smiled. "That bastard is doing twenty-five years, mom," Amber said happily and ran to call her Uncle Mauricio. "Girl, hush your mouth with that kind of talk. Now, what did you say Priscilla? Well, thank you Lord. That is good to hear. I wish it was life, but you can only get what you are supposed to get," Leslie says as she prepares lunch for the girls.

"Did you tell Cheyanne yet because she will know if you just mistakenly told Amber. It is okay if it comes from her best friend. She is over here and about to eat lunch. I will do disaster control if need be. Love you, girl. See you later!" Leslie hangs up the phone with a smile on her face and tears in her eyes. "Now, it really begins. He will get exactly what he gave!" Leslie mumbles to herself as she finishes making the girls' lunches.

Cheyanne took the news quite well. For some reason, she told Amber that her spirit sat well with the outcome. If he truly did the things that they say he did, then he deserves what he gets. Amber was happy to see that Cheyanne did not realize she was the girl that they spoke of on the news, and it did not bother her that people knew her uncle was not only a drug dealer and a fraudster but also a pedophile. They sat in Amber's room and played with each other's hair until Leslie told them to wash up for lunch. They were trying to figure out how to wear their hair for Wednesday and especially for prom. They already

had an appointment to have their dresses fitted and made in the East Village at ENZ's.

Wednesday came and the girls were so excited and so were Benjamin and Dillon. The mutual relationships between the four had been pretty good up until the point when they heard about the death of their classmate, Duncan. Amber even had a few conversations with Morales about everything that happened since they had broken up. They decided being friends was better than being enemies. Even though Morales could not trust Amber as far as he could throw her, he tried to put his love and crushed feelings aside and be her friend again. It was going okay from both of their perspectives. He liked that she was back in his life even though she had a boyfriend, but he planned on eliminating his competition somehow and some way.

There were cameras and news people everywhere. The gym seemed to be filled to capacity. There were college and university flags and paraphernalia all over the gym. The DJ was playing music, and the people were just so excited for what was about to happen. The crew were four of twenty people who were going to sign Letters of Intent that afternoon. It would be live on ESPN3 and the seniors were dressed to impress. Their parents did not look too bad themselves. Amber's dad, Felton, even flew in from Pittsburgh. She also asked Nicholai to come to the signing. He was almost a part of her family now. Her twin little brothers, Isaiah and Xavier, were running around with the other students' siblings. It was a sight to see in the gym of Towson Catholic High.

As the announcer went through each student one by one and they declared where they intended to go and signed, the crowd went crazier and crazier. A few boos did happen when people were disappointed that a student chose one school over another, but all seemed to go well. It was Dillon's turn, and he had two hats sitting in front of him—Syracuse and Rutgers. Dillon stood up. The recruiters from Syracuse and Rutgers were on their toes. Both of their letters were sitting in front of him. He hugged his mother and gave Benjamin a bro-hug. "I have decided to go to Ohio State!" Dillon says as the crowd goes haywire, and his mom places the cap on his head. The Ohio State recruiter stepped over to where he was and shook his hand as he smiled at the other recruiters. "Well, what a coincidence, Dillon," Benjamin says as he stands up because I am not going to Syracuse, Rutgers, or Penn State. I am also going to Ohio State to play football and basketball!" By this time, the crowd completely lost it. The Rutgers and Syracuse recruiters left the gym quickly. The ESPN3 announcer was literally in tears from laughing.

Amber went over and hugged Benjamin. Then, she returned to her seat. Cheyanne followed suit. They smiled and looked at each other. "Well, I guess we have a somewhat similar situation," Amber grabbed the hand of her best friend. "You are right. We do, Amber," Cheyanne exclaimed. "Cheyanne and I have decided to take our track talents to Xavier University to pursue our education as pharmacists!" Amber said as she and Cheyanne signed their letters simultaneously. The crowd and their parents were very ecstatic, and there were hugs all around. They already knew that the girls were going to school together.

This was a plan from the time that they had declared that they would be BFF's forever. This was just the beginning of their tremendous future together.

Chapter 15

"I am so excited because it almost time for prom," Amber exclaimed as she tried on the dress in ENZ's. "We are going to go to prom and then it is off to graduation!" Cheyanne yelled through the wall of the dressing room. They both came out of their dressing rooms and screamed together. They looked so beautiful in their matching dresses. They were both two pieces, all bejeweled with Swartz diamonds on the top and a flare to the skirt bottom; but Cheyanne's was a candy apple red and Amber's was a teal blue. They wanted the same dress but to not be the same color. The guys were next door trying on their suits that had matching candy apple and teal blue cumber buns and ties. The suits were white, and the shoes were the same color as the girls' dresses also. They looked so fresh from head to toe. The excitement was so thick that the foursome could cut it with a knife.

After their shopping trip on the East Side, the crew headed out for a double date lunch at Sushi Seki. The ladies were quite surprised about being taken here because they saw on Yelp that it was very expensive. But they did not complain at all because they were used to being pampered and spoiled by their parents. So why should they not expect that from their boyfriends? The girls laughed to themselves as the guys ordered for them and conversed with each other about their upcoming visit to Ohio State before graduation. They were just as silly as two little schoolgirls walking pass their crush. Amber and Cheyanne found this to be very cute. They enjoyed being in relationships with the

most popular guys in school, and to boot, they treated them as ladies and not like the hoodrats that attended their school.

Lunch was very nice and Benjamin drove everyone home in his Camaro. Amber and Cheyanne went to her house and chilled inside watching movies on Amber's Amazon Firestick. Mauricio came from Haiti to help prepare Amber for prom. He promised her from the time she was in kindergarten that he would be there for his only great niece's prom. She was, in fact, the only girl on both sides of her family. He father had six sons from another woman, and her mother only had her and her twin brothers. It was quite something for Amber, especially being the oldest either way.

"She will be the one to set the bar for her brothers" is what her grandmother Ann Marie would always say. Ann Marie always spoke so highly of Amber to everyone in Atlanta and Haiti. There was not anyone that knew her that did not know about Amber and all of her accomplishments. The thought of her grandmother made her smile as she lay on her bed watching television and stroking the charm on the gold necklace that Ann Marie gave her when she was born. It was solid gold cross with her name and date of birth engraved on it. Cheyanne tickled Amber when she saw her lying there smiling. She was happy that all was well with their lives at this moment.

June was finally here as finals and the last grades of their high school career had been turned in. Yearbooks were being signed and final goodbyes to their teachers and underclassmen were being said. What a year it had been in high school, and the seniors who survived

were ever so grateful that they did. There had been many losses this year, but there had also been many gains—many friendships and bonds that would last forever. Prom was one day away and graduation was in three. The seniors literally broke the doors down trying to leave school on June 1, and there was no stopping them. Some went to the mall for last-minute shopping for prom, while others went to get their hair and nails done. The guys went to get a haircut so they could just sleep all day until the parties before prom.

Amber and Cheyanne went to the nail salon. Their hair appointments were not until tomorrow. They wanted them to be extra fresh for the prom. They did not want to risk sleeping on the hairdo and waking up looking like trolls. They sat and chatted while getting their pedicures done. Some other girls from their school walked in and gave them the side eye. They were not part of the "in" crowd, but they were known as the so-called mean girls. Cheyanne and Amber did not pay them any attention. They started talking about Amber and Cheyanne and making jokes about them. One girl even walked by and bumped the chair that Amber was in. "I usually do not speak on the dead, but did they not hear about the behind whooping I gave Rayland when she stepped to me about my man in my yard?" Amber asked Cheyanne very loudly so everyone could hear.

"They must have not heard or else they would not start no crap because we will dog walk these chicks the day before prom and still look better than all of them put together," Cheyanne said in her strongest Bajan accent. It kind of scared Amber at first when she heard

her speak. Cheyanne always tried her best to control her accent. But she continued giving the girls the death stare and they left them alone.

"I wonder what the hell that was all about?" Cheyanne asked Amber as they left the nail salon. "I do not know, but they made the right move by shutting up and sitting down somewhere," Amber stated while looking at her newly manicured nails. "They wanted an end o' high school butt kicking. I would have been happy to oblige them," Amber laughed as they crossed the street to the parking garage to her new 2016 pearl-colored CLS400 Mercedes-Benz.

She got this car as a gift from her dad for graduating a valedictorian. Her parents were very proud of her. Cheyanne was getting a car also but she had to wait until the summer when her dad came back from Barbados. He would miss graduation but she understood. He was there taking care of her ailing grandmother.

The following day came so quickly. The girls felt as if they had not slept at all. Their hair appointment was at eleven in the morning and their party before the prom was at three in the afternoon. Prom was at six in the evening, and they were too ready for the time to go quickly. They got their hair done, and their families came together at Amber's house. They helped decorate and get ready for all of the other couples to arrive in their cars and wait to be picked up after the party by their limos or leave in their rentals. Amber and Cheyanne put on their pre-prom outfits and greeted the guests. Everyone looked wonderful as they walked the red carpet that led to the patio and had

their pictures taken as they approached the entrance. The party was such a great time with appetizers, picture taking, and even more yearbook signings. It was around 5:15 p.m. when the limos started to arrive to pick up the seniors to take them to their prom at the Waldorf Astoria. Amber and Cheyanne then decided it was time to freshen up their makeup and get dressed so that they could take their pictures with their ever so handsome dates and leave for the prom.

The foursome's parents were so thrilled at the sight of the well-dressed teenagers. They all looked at them and could not believe that their children were about to go not only to prom but also, in the next two days, to be walking across the stage to receive their high school diplomas. The parents all beamed with such pride and love in their eyes. They were so overjoyed that their children made it through all of the chaos that happened during their senior year and that it had not caused them lasting pain.

A Hummersine pulled up and the foursome got into after taking a million pictures with each other and their families. They made their way to the hotel. It was a beautiful sight to see. When they entered the hotel, it was like entering a golden castle with crystals and chandeliers at every turn. The ballroom was immense and pulsating music that the walls felt they were sending vibrations through the kids' bodies. The prom was already at full swing, and it was just 6:00 p.m. Everyone was arriving around the same time and signing the guest book. They went straight to the dance floor without finding their tables. The principal encouraged the seniors to find their tables and

prepare for the presentation of awards and the crowning of the King and Queen so that they could enjoy the dance.

Everyone eventually found their seats and sat down. The principal gave a very moving speech about transitioning into college life, which took fifteen minutes and almost put the seniors to sleep. When she noticed that she was losing them, she then called the student council to the stage to announce the Prom King and Queen. Student Council secretary Michelle Hawthorne came to the stage and called the names of the candidates for King and Queen. They all lined up including Amber, Benjamin, Cheyanne, and Dillon. They were all pumped and ready to get it over with so they could dance some more. "The winners of the Towson Catholic High School 2015-2016 Senior Prom King and Queen titles are Dillon Parks and Cheyanne Louis!" The seniors went crazy as they crowned Cheyanne and Dillon. Amber and Benjamin were so happy for them. They already had their turn at being king and queen so their friends being crowned meant the world to them. "It's time to party!" Cheyanne yelled taking the microphone from Michelle. The seniors partied until midnight.

Sleeping was all most of the seniors did after prom. They not only partied at prom, but most of them had after-parties upstairs in the penthouse suites at the Waldorf Astoria or went to the teenage club for Amber's party. Nicholai paid to have it shut down and only opened to the seniors who received invitations from Amber and Cheyanne. They had a great time and did not get home until around 5:00 a.m. The girls went home and slept until 4:00 p.m. the next day. They ate a late lunch and went to the mall. They had dinner with Benjamin and his family

and went back home to sleep some more. Everyone was pooped but still stoked about the next day being graduation.

Graduation was being held at Onondaga War Memorial at 6:00 p.m. The seniors of Tucson Catholic High School were patiently waiting in the foyer as their families franticly looked for seats. There were tears and flowers. There were hugs and high fives. No one was more nervous than Amber. Her speech was all she could think about in her head. If she only knew what her future would hold for her, she might have just ran away to a foreign country and forget everything right then and there.

Everyone was finally seated and the graduates entered the auditorium. They stood for the Pledge of Allegiance, and the Star-Spangled Banner was sung by Cheyanne while she fought back tears. The chorus sang the class song *Wind Beneath My Wings*, and most of the parents in the auditorium broke down like babies. "Now for our valedictorian, Amber Hollingsworth," the principal said and Amber took the stage.

"Good evening, my name is Amber Hollingsworth and I would like to thank all of you for coming to celebrate the graduation of Towson Catholic High School's 2016 senior class. It has occurred to me that the last twelve to thirteen years together have been like the books that we have all read. Those years have skipped ahead to an event that seemed to be off in the distance but is now here today.

We had our introductions in middle school because I transferred here from Atlanta, the rising action of the plot throughout

high school, the climax of senior year, and now we are at our resolution with graduation. Today is not just an ending. It is also the beginning of the new volume that we will be writing.

Some of us unfortunately did not make it to graduation. Some of us did not even get a chance to go to the Grad Bash or even our Senior Prom. We are the author of our own stories and today our Volume 1: The Formative Years has ended. As the Class of 2017, we turn the final page together. We await what will be written next with bright, blank pages before us.

Now, we can reflect on past chapters to help us write our future volumes. In Chapter 1: Our Childhood, we went through grade school and learned lessons like 'sharing is caring,' the golden rule, don't take candy from strangers and no budging in the lunch line—which, by the way, never seemed to sink in. We also learned to make new friends while keeping the old. This chapter also had its challenges of learning basic math and telling time on an analog clock, those were rough times. Chapter 2 was the in-between years where we were thirteen and acted like we were twenty. We thought we knew everything. Yeah, we had lots of swag. But somehow we learned to balance our emotions as we transitioned from our childhood to our teenage years. It was only in middle school where school dances were a big deal. We would be excited for months in advance and plan our outfits weeks before. We were exposed to the awkward "boy likes girl, girl is 2 feet taller than boy, but just didn't matter." It was such a traumatic and difficult stage.

Chapter 3: The High School Teenager is where each year's homework got increasingly harder, but we still found time to display our school pride. Go, Bulldogs! During these past four years, our time management has improved not only to accommodate our school load but to account for work and time with friends. Now, as we head into the upcoming chapters, we bring what we have learned, our friends, and also the memories with us, so that wherever we go making the bad times tolerable and the good times better. Not every chapter will be light reading; there will be struggles. I leave you with this Class of 2017—never stop writing. Congratulations, Class of 2017! We made it!"

Amber's speech without any trouble, and she spoke so eloquently. She received a standing ovation, and she cried all the way back to her seat.

****

"Dad! He won't stop screaming!" Amber yelled to Felton as she tried to stop Joshua from screaming. He bit her. She slapped him. Felton dropped his body weight on Joshua and put a hold on his neck. "Stop moving you jerk. It won't be long before you bleed out," Felton says as he slowly removes his body from Joshua's. Joshua stayed still and began coughing up a little blood. "If you let me die, you won't know where I have Cheyanne," Joshua says almost out of breath. "She came here because she found out I was planning to have your ass killed. She was going to call the police. But I hid her away. So if you let me die, she will run out of air and die." Amber fell to her knees and

began to cry hysterically. Felton made a call. "Tex, this Legs. I need you to get over here now. Bring your medical kit."

Made in the USA
Columbia, SC
28 June 2020